Lions

The Secret of Hunter's Keep

Daniel pressed his face into the ground. His hands were hidden. He hoped that he merged with the dark. He held his breath, and tried desperately to telepath the foxcub.

"Don't move. Don't whimper. Don't breathe."

"Black as a coal mine. Might be a good idea to block it. There are those cut logs on the other side of the ride."

Daniel lay still, horrified. They were going to seal him up. He ought to cry out. He couldn't. His voice wouldn't work. Maybe he could move the logs when the men had gone. He watched as the entrance grew smaller and smaller and finally there was nothing but the stifling dark that enclosed him with its choking smell.

Also available in Lions

THE SECRET OF HUNTER'S KEEP

Joyce Stranger

Lions
An Imprint of HarperCollinsPublishers

First published in Great Britain in Lions in 1993

1 3 5 7 9 10 8 6 4 2

Lions is an imprint of HarperCollins Children's Books,
a division of HarperCollins Publishers Ltd, 77-85 Fulham Palace
Road, Hammersmith, London W6 8JB

ISBN 0 00 674738 8

Printed and bound in Great Britain
by HarperCollins Book Manufacturing Ltd, Glasgow

Chapter One

"Keep still, don't move. Not even a whisper."
Jake Leigh's words were hissed very softly. The
children huddled behind the fallen tree, trembling with excitement. Jake, who was warden of
the Wildfowl Sanctuary, had promised to take
them fox-watching two years ago. This was the
first time that the promise had been kept.

"Look there!" he said, pointing to the path
that led to the worked-out stone quarry. "Feathers. He's been killing."

The little telltale pile told more to Daniel
Murray than to Anna Colley. Daniel's father
was the old Lord's Head Gamekeeper. The only
gamekeeper now, in fact, but he still had the
title.

Anna, whose father farmed the land that ran
alongside the woods, thought it was one of her
father's Rhode Island Reds. Daniel knew it was
one of his father's precious pheasants.

Blacktip had signed his own death warrant.

"Look," Jake said. "There, where the path
breaks through the brambles to the lip of the

quarry. You can just see the darkness of the cave. It's part of an old badger working, deep in the bank at the edge of the stone. A maze of tunnels. It's not Blacktip who dens there; it's the vixen. She has five cubs."

His voice was very soft, scarcely more than a breath on the wind and the children had to listen intently to hear him. Even the faintest sound would keep the vixen underground.

"Blacktip helps feed them, but he has a den under a hollow tree, at the far side of the wood. He is often around in the early evening. The vixen comes out later. She isn't due for another fifteen minutes at least."

Jake spent many nights watching the wild animals and knew the paths that all of them took, when they had young, and where they played and fed. He was part of the badger patrol that watched over the setts to try and ensure that no men came digging with terriers to kill the animals.

He glanced at his luminous watch.

"She'll be out very soon. Don't even breathe," he whispered.

There was a brilliant moon, the light dappling the woods, and the edge of the quarry was easily seen.

Daniel felt an insane desire to sneeze. He was

worried about the vixen as she was on his Lordship's land, and the old man wouldn't tolerate foxes near his pheasants. Why couldn't she have made her den in the sanctuary? But then Jake's wildfowl would have been at risk as well as the other creatures that sheltered there.

She isn't safe and they aren't safe, he thought. The Lord owned all the woods and the big house where Daniel lived with his family in the only surviving wing. Jake Leigh lived in the old stable block, in a flat that had once belonged to the Head Groom. The Lord and his family lived in a large modern house at the edge of the woods. The mansion was semi-derelict, most of the rooms open to the wind and the rain and the stars. It had been hit by a bomb at the end of World War II, and so much damage had been done that repair was impossible. Nature had taken over, so that in places it was difficult to tell what had been inside and what was outside, except for the half-standing walls and remains of window and door frames. It was a wonderful place to play.

Both children knew of the priesthole behind the priesthole; only Daniel knew of the tunnel that led from the wing where his family lived, under the house, through the cellars and out in the basin of the long-derelict fountain, its entrance hidden by a mass of Russian vine.

He slipped through it at night when his parents thought he was sleeping. Sometimes he shadowed Jake, but was careful not to be seen or his excursions would be stopped. They might even nail up the tunnel entrance in his room. He could never get close enough to the animals Jake watched, but he did see Blacktip slip along the pathways, and sometimes heard the badgers foraging.

He dared not do it often in case he was caught.

He had found the passage by accident, tripping and falling. He put out a hand to save himself and grasped the head of one of the carved swans that ornamented the mantelpiece.

The fireplace swung away and he stared at a black gap in the wall, at steps leading downwards into the fusty, earth-smelling dark. He explored the tunnel system for months before he found the old exit in the basin of the fountain in the grounds.

He had not used it tonight. Jake had permission to take them fox-watching, though Daniel suspected his father intended to discover, next day, what they had seen. It was no use hoping that a gamekeeper wouldn't know where the vixen laired or that she had cubs. The men with their guns went out every year and every year Daniel agonised.

It was only a matter of time before the vixen was shot. He could do nothing to stop it and had learned, long ago, not to argue with his father. He could not bear the icy silence or the angry looks. He learned to shoot at clay pigeons to keep the family peace. A son who would not use a gun was unthinkable. Daniel beat at the shoots, but was careful to ensure that none of the birds he flushed were ever killed by the guns. Jake hated the shoots too. His birds were never shot and many of the pheasants flew into the sanctuary, aware that no gun ever spoke there.

It was odd, Daniel often thought, that the old Lord could keep Daniel's father busy with the pheasants, and shoot them every year, and yet employ Jake to keep the sanctuary safe for the birds and geese and the animals that laired there.

"Killing animals and birds doesn't mean you don't respect them," his father said. "Those of us who live in the country have to learn what is sensible and what is not. It doesn't do to kill for the fun of it. I know how many birds can be taken each year. Jake and I are opposite sides of

9

the same coin and even Jake realises that no land can have more beasts and fowl than can be fed from it."

Jake hated the cull of foxes, even though they sometimes took his wildfowl.

No one could hunt on horseback in this type of country. It was steep and rocky, leg breaking for horses. The foxes hid in the wilderness on the hills, and men and terriers hunted them on foot.

Daniel's father rounded up the farmers every year. One spring they killed seventy foxes on one day. No land could stand so many. There was only enough food for half that number, so that the farmers' hens suffered, and any sickly lambs. The old foxes died of starvation, unable to hunt, and sometimes the cubs died too, as the vixens had not enough food for milk. Keeping the numbers down meant that those that survived were well nourished.

Daniel knew that, but he still hated the killing. He eased his cramped leg. Would the vixen never come?

There was a soft skitter. The moon rode high in a cloudless sky. Bright stars glittered above them.

It was early May. Only a few days left of the Easter holidays, otherwise the children would not have been allowed out in the middle of the night.

Jake crawled forward to the quarry edge, and looked down. He was almost invisible, dressed in brown cords and a camouflage jacket, a cap pulled well down over his eyes. He had told each child what to wear. Anna was in dark green and Daniel had borrowed his father's working jacket, which was green and brown camouflage.

It was far too big but his own anorak was brilliantly coloured in red and scarlet and blue. His mother liked bright colours and could not understand a son who wanted to dress drably.

His mother insisted, tonight, that he dressed warmly even though the night was mild. She did not know about his other excursions.

Jake knew and warned him repeatedly, disapproving. At times Jake could be as irritating as any other grown-up.

An owl hooted. The soft mournful call died away and was answered from the other side of the woods. A faint ghost of a bird sailed over their heads, white wings silent.

Jake signalled to the children, his slowly moving hand saying "Watch".

They crept towards him, scarcely daring to breathe.

"Look out for broken twigs; one snap and they'll be off, faster than snow under the summer sun," Jake had said several times, drilling it into

11

them. Slowly, slowly, watch the ground. Don't make a sound.

Daniel reached him first and looked down.

He was aware of Anna close to him, her breathing sounding too loud.

There was mud at the edge of the slope, and deep prints where the dog fox had run, carrying his catch to the vixen. The quarry had been worked out long ago. Grass and bramble, briar and thorn grew thickly, hiding the cut surfaces.

"The stone was used to build the mansion," Anna's great-grandfather said. He had been Head Stableman, at the time of the First World War. He was ninety-three but could still joke and talk with them and tell them of the days when there had been hunts and balls, and grand dinners and parties.

The king and queen had visited, once. That had been a carry-on, he said, everyone dressed in their best, everywhere painted and decorated afresh, huge hampers of food brought in to eat. Hurrying and scurrying and flurrying, and the old Lord's father yelling at them all, so that they put on a good show. The old Lord was the young Lord then.

"Wild man, the old Lord's father was when he was sober; terrifying when he was drunk, an absolute devil," the old man said. "Worse than his son – and he's a tartar. He's a lamb by comparison with his dad." The children were very glad the old Lord's father had died before they were born.

"That unlucky bomb was a wicked shame. Destroyed everything, not only the mansion. A way of life went with it."

Daniel watched the bushes, but nothing moved. He was hungry and annoyingly remembered Nat Colley's description of the preparations for the royal feast.

"Salmon and grouse and pheasant, venison and partridge and quail. Exotic fruits and vegetables and the cooks terrified lest their food was spoiled. Jellies and trifles and mousses. A meringue in the shape of a swan. You never saw anything like it. I peeked through the windows. Silver and glass and gold."

He brought the place to life for the children who listened, enthralled.

Daniel tried to control his wandering thoughts. He could feel cold stone under his hands. It was covered in wet lichen. He was scarcely aware of it. All his mind was concentrated on the shiver in the grass below them.

"One move, and she'll be off," Jake warned them before they set out. "You must be as still as a hare. You know the countryman's way of telling that a tump in a field is a hare?"

The children shook their heads. They adored Jake. He was gentle, with a quirky sense of humour and had an immense fund of knowledge which he was always eager to share. He had time for them. Their parents were so busy.

"If it moves, it's a cowpat. If it's so still you think it's a stone, then it's a hare."

Daniel grinned. Anna, who found it hard to see a joke, merely stared at Jake, puzzled.

Would the vixen come? Daniel had often seen her in the distance, a lean grey shape, a black bar on either side of her muzzle, so that he named her Blackface. Blacktip had the black at the end of his splendid red brush. Daniel was used to meeting both foxes and a third who sometimes ventured into the woods. They stood to watch him, eyes glowing, one paw raised, doglike, before loping on, sure he posed no threat to them.

The old badger at the far side of the wood often crossed the path too, grunting to himself as he went.

Daniel had not seen Blackface since the cubs were born. Four weeks old, Jake thought.

The quarryside was empty. It was hard to believe that there was any creature alive. Then, very slowly, a pointed muzzle peeped out of the

14

brambles and sniffed the air. Jake had been careful to judge the wind. No scent would blow to her from them.

"If you had noses like hers, you'd smell her," Jake said, when he positioned them.

Lean shoulders followed the pointed head. The black bars were vivid against her white cheeks. Pointed ears moved, questioning the wind, listening for telltale sounds that forecast danger. Far away a car revved and hooted and the vixen was gone, the quarry empty, as if she had never been there at all.

Jake signalled to them to lie still.

"She's moving," he whispered in Daniel's ear. "I saw her head briefly as she sniffed the wind."

Excitement built in him as he watched. This time he saw the pricked ears, the questing nose, lifted, sniffing for news of enemies on the wind.

A car on the motorway revved as it overtook a vehicle and hooted, loud and clear. Again the head vanished.

Daniel had never been so disappointed in his life.

"What now?" he asked, his voice as low as Jake's.

"We wait," Jake said. "And we hope."

The endless minutes crept slowly on, and the little trio lay quiet, nothing moving but their eyes.

Chapter Two

Owl call and rustle in the undergrowth as some tiny creature moved. Mouse or shrew, or maybe a weasel. The faraway roar of traffic on the motorway, a ceaseless background of noise that the animals learned to ignore. So long as no car hooted.

A cow on Anna's father's farm suddenly bellowed for the bull. She would be noisy all night, but her din posed no threat to the foxes.

Daniel held his breath.

They couldn't lie there for hours and see nothing. She must come. Please let her come. He looked up at the moon above him, that watched and saw so much. Lucky moon.

Daniel did not see her come.

One moment the ground was bare, and the next the vixen was in the little clearing where the cut stone formed a platform before dropping again to watery deeps that reflected a full moon. Hunter's moon, Daniel knew. Hunter's moon over Hunter's Keep. He loved the name of the old house as much as he loved the house and its memories.

There would be a full moon tomorrow as well. Perhaps it would rain. If his father realised the pheasant had been killed . . . If only Blacktip had taken just the one, and not stopped to kill for the sheer fun of it. Foxes will be foxes, Jake often said. Daniel intended to get up early and reach the pheasant pens first and see what damage had been done. Perhaps he could hide the telltale signs before his father arrived.

The old Lord valued his pheasants and was furious if any creature took one. He even wanted Ken Murray to kill the buzzards that sometimes took a chick.

"Protecting birds! Killers, the lot of them. Never heard such nonsense in my life." His voice boomed across the room. The Lord was prepared to conserve anything of value to himself and get rid of everything else. He railed at Daniel's father, who refused to break the law.

Wild birds could not be shot. Foxes were different.

If his father knew the pheasants were being taken he would use his gun, and Anna's father would join him. Jack Colley had lost three geese in the last two weeks. They would collect the three farmers from down the valley.

The old Lord didn't tolerate children either. He was a big man, fierce blue eyes under shaggy white brows stared from a red face. His thick white hair gleamed like silk, but the big moustache was yellowed. He strode along at an incredible pace for so old a man, swishing a long stick that Anna said contained a sword. He slashed the heads off the flowers, and hit out at the tree trunks and the fences, as if they had injured him and he needed to take revenge.

"He'd run us through for tuppence," Anna said, scaring herself.

He shook the stick at the children whenever he saw them.

"Go away, little horrors. Get away!" His voice was thunderous, frightening them. Sometimes Daniel thought his father was afraid of the Lord and he knew his mother dreaded the old man's visits. He called to make sure that all the arrangements had been made for the shoots in the autumn months.

Daniel's father spent hours checking every detail.

"Your father is preparing for everything that could go wrong including the sky falling," his mother said, after one particularly fraught evening when neither of them dared say one word.

Daniel, lying so still, waiting and watching, wished he could control his thoughts.

As the cubs came out into the moonlight he hated all of the men. The tiny animals didn't deserve to die. They enchanted him.

Within moments they were playing, reminding Daniel of the litters of pups that his father bred. A gamekeeper could never rely on his wages – they were so low. The old Lord needed the money from the shoots to keep himself and his family. The pheasants were his. The pups brought in welcome extra cash for Daniel's family. Provided the jam on their bread and marge, his mother said. She cared for the puppies, and loved them, and hated it when they were sold.

Snipe, the best spaniel they had ever had, had a litter the same age as these cubs.

They rolled together. Two of them found a piece of rag and each tugged at it until it tore, leaving both victors. They soon tired and dropped their trophies. One curled up to sleep and the other picked up a stick and carried it proudly, the effort to swagger marred by its unsteady gait. Another discovered a beetle walking on the ground and nosed it, fascinated, but did not know what to do about his find. The vixen, seeing him, darted across, and killed and ate. She moved like a dancing cat.

The smallest of the cubs, a little female with a more pointed muzzle than the rest, with her mother's black bars on either side of her nose, found a feather. It blew in the wind. She danced after it and tumbled and fell. Her brother stalked and pranced and she attacked him, snarling and growling, biting at his legs and tail in an effort to regain her prize.

The vixen snapped at them, stopping the quarrel. A moment later it was forgotten and they chased one another through the brambles, playing hide and seek, darting out at one another, as yet unsteady on their paws, so that they often fell.

Anna sighed with delight. Tomorrow she would draw them. Her fingers itched to start but she had not dared to bring a sketch book. She had to lie still.

One of the dog cubs, bigger than the others, went off on his own, exploring. Within seconds he was too near the slope. The vixen, ever alert, ran to him, seized him in her jaws, carried him back to his litter mates and dumped him unceremoniously on the grass.

Irritated, he yapped at her, a small defiance that made the children grin. She nipped him. He whimpered and licked at his paw. She rolled and in a moment the cubs were at her, sucking from her, as she lay under the moon.

None of them saw the sleek shape that approached them from behind. He barked, a sharp sound of warning, and in seconds the quarry was deserted. Daniel turned his head, and for a moment he and Blacktip gazed eye to eye, and then the fox was gone, melting into the darkness.

"We'll see no more tonight," Jake said. He stood and stretched.

The children, following him, yawned, longing for bed. Daniel glanced at his watch: 2 a.m. Very late, even for him. He always made sure he was home from his illicit excursions by midnight.

Jake saw them safely home before returning to his own vigil, afraid that Blacktip might come to the sanctuary and take more of his geese and ducks. Three pairs of swans were breeding, and their eggs would be at risk. It was the first time that the visiting swans had bred.

Daniel, lying in his bed, watched the moon slip down the sky. He thought of the cubs. The big one, in particular, was so puppylike with his fluffy coat and waddling walk, falling once or twice as he tried to run.

If only he could have a fox cub of his own. A

friend of his father's, a gamekeeper on another estate, had once had a tame foxcub, which one his terriers had brought home alive and suckled with her own puppies.

"Crazy," Ken Murray said.

The cub had grown to full size, and then escaped one night. It had been a delightful little animal. Daniel had only been seven years old at the time and he had adored it. One of the farmers had also found a cub alive after the vixen had been shot and taken it home with them. It had played with his Labradors and slept with them on the hearthrug.

A little vixen, she had vanished when she was about nine months old, looking for a mate.

Live and let live, Jake said, understanding them, when Ken Murray told him, angry at what he termed their idiocy.

Daniel thought of the Lord's fury if he knew that a cub was being kept as pet; of his father's anger, and of Anna's father's rage.

To them the foxes were vermin. They were breeding far too many cubs and it was not easy for the men to find time to hunt them and shoot them. It needed so much planning and every den had to be noted.

If only his father didn't notice that the pheasant had gone . . .

Daniel slept and fear stalked his dreams. Fear of a wild old man who chased him yelling, a sword gleaming in his hand; and of other men with guns who fanned out on the hill and shot, again and again and again until no creature was left to walk the woods at night. He was no longer a boy, but a running fox, desperate for life, with enemies all around him.

Chapter Three

Daniel woke as his mother shook him. She put the plate of toast and the cup of coffee down on his bedside table.

"Your father's angry. You promised to feed the pups for him this morning. Listen to them."

Hungry pups squealed. Daniel didn't know why they hadn't wakened him. He leapt out of bed, promising himself a proper wash later. He ate as he dressed, and hurtled into the kitchen, on his way to the back door.

"Hair," his mother said. "You aren't going out like that. And don't talk about foxes. Three more birds went in the night."

Daniel brushed savagely at the dark curls. Time it was cut. He hated it long, and insisted that it lay short and sleek without a hint of wave. He plastered it with gel, and combed it through again, not satisfied until every tiny kink had been flattened.

"Foxes, not poachers?" he asked his mother, waiting for her approving nod as she looked at him.

"Poachers don't leave bones and feathers."

Another night raid. There would be an avenging army. Three birds a night for just sixty nights meant one hundred and eighty dead pheasants. The vixens were hungry, and he knew there were at least four within a ten-mile radius. There could be more.

Once they discovered the pheasants were easy prey they would be back again and again. Too many of the birds died on the roads, and no one could do anything about that. The silly creatures were prize jay walkers, with no traffic sense at all, often crossing right in front of an approaching car, giving the driver no time at all to dodge them.

He had been out with Jake when one hit the Land Rover, and flew on, leaving a cloud of feathers in the air. Dan looked for a bald bird and Jake laughed.

"He'll have a sore head. Just got rid of some loose plumage – won't even notice," he said.

Jake had seen four dog foxes together, in early March, at Mile End. The postman had seen five at the Southeys. Foxes didn't usually congregate. There were only five miles between the two sightings. Nine foxes; and Blackface had five cubs. How many more cubs in the area? All with mouths that needed feeding.

His mother had weighed the puppy food. Every dog had its own dish, and each had the amount it needed according to its weight. Daniel's father hated fat animals. Labradors and spaniels both tended to overeat unless carefully controlled. Overweight dogs couldn't work, and were more likely to be ill. He took the tray of dishes across to the big whelping kennel. Snipe greeted him with frantically waving stumpy tail. Her own food waited on the bench under the window. She fed alone, as the pups stole from her and made her angry. She growled at them.

It had been easier before they were weaned.

Dan imagined her saying, "My food, mine, you little horrors. Let me eat in peace." She was savagely hungry. The pups had taken so much of her energy. She was starvation thin, her coat glaring, not at all like her usual sleek self. The pups were now a burden, not a pleasure, and their small teeth hurt when they playbit her paws and ears.

They learned to respect her, as she turned on them, telling them to leave her alone. As soon as they obeyed she forgave them, cuddled them close and licked them, showing how much she appreciated well-behaved puppies, but would not tolerate little villains.

"Watch her," Ken Murray said, giving Daniel

a lesson in dog handling. "Instant displeasure and immediate praise. She knows how a puppy thinks."

So why grumble at me all the time and never praise me when I've done right? Daniel thought. I need approval too, just like the dogs. Jake was always quick to thank.

"You did that well. Be easier next time, though," he'd say. Daniel could accept that, but not constant criticism that made him feel useless. It wasn't worth trying at times.

"Your father likes everything done splendidly," his mother said, after one particularly disastrous meal, when the potatoes were hard and the meat tough. She had been out all morning creosoting coops and had cooked in a hurry. The Lord had called in too, just before lunch and kept her talking. "He doesn't mean to grumble all the time. He's tired, too. Too many poachers at night, and no other keepers now. You have to make allowances, Daniel."

Why? Daniel felt rebellious. He had problems too and nobody ever listened to him or cared about his needs. There were times when he wondered if his parents remembered he existed.

He wished he could switch off his own memory.

Seven little dishes. Seven small eager mouths.

He placed them well apart, as the boss pup ate fast and stole from his brothers and sisters. Daniel stayed in the kennel, watching them eat, ready to make sure nobody got more than a fair share.

The smallest bitch was slow and he protected her plate for her, fending off the other pups who bullied and teased her. She leaned against his leg, valuing his presence.

"Last time you go fox-watching at night, my lad," his father said, looking through the kennel door. "I said six o'clock, not seven. There's too much to do to lie in bed idling."

There was always too much to do and the old Lord had no time for laggards. Coops to mend and coops to creosote; pens to make and pens to move. Birds to dose when they were ill. Chicks to rear and eggs to protect. Nests to guard and nests to find. One man trying to do work that had once been done by five.

Always the constant war on the ground on rat and stoat and weasel, on fox and mink. Tish, Daniel's Jack Russell, kept the rats in check, aided by his father's pair, Tinker and Torment.

There was also danger from the air. Kestrel and sparrowhawk, marauding crows, and even the magpies that could spear a little chick and fly away with it.

Now there was a new danger. The circling bird in the sky caught Daniel's eye. He held his breath, praying that his father hadn't seen it. A red kite. He knew they had been released near by and his father was angry. As if there weren't enough birds preying on his precious stock. He hated the breeding programmes that released predators to hunt, especially when they hunted on his patch.

The bird soared over the Hump, a scrubby hill that separated the Lord's land from Anna's father's farm. It swung down the wind and vanished and Daniel released his breath. His father was busy in the food store. He emerged blinking in the bright sunlight.

"Put the pups in the pen."

I have to say please, so why don't you? Daniel thought irritably. He watched his father walk across the yard, two of the black Labradors at his heels. Ken was proud of the Sandringham blood in them. His ambition was to sell a dog to the Queen, who could handle a gundog as well as any of her keepers.

These two dogs were called Perca and Brama, the perch and the bream. Ken Murray named his Labradors after fish and his spaniels after birds. Grouse, one of the younger springers, was due to whelp in a few days' time.

Spring litter, long evenings, plenty of time for training, his father said. Only daft animals give birth in winter. No Christmas litters for him, and his pups were only sold to people whom he questioned mercilessly.

"No use selling a working springer as a pet. Recipe for disaster." He said it so often that Daniel worried if he saw a springer spaniel on a lead in town, a 'walk to the post box and back to the hearthrug' dog. His father's dogs had endless exercise, running, swimming, walking. They needed to be fit for the shooting season.

Anna, appearing from behind the kennel, walked towards him. Her mass of red curls burned in the sunlight.

"Ten of Dad's hens dead. He took two and left the rest with their heads bitten off."

"Have you come to entice Daniel away for your own purposes?" Ken Murray asked. Anna and Daniel occasionally appeared to share their homes. Both were only children and behaved like brother and sister, they knew one another so well.

"Dad says OK for tonight," Anna said. "And there's a message from Jake. His mother is ill. She's had an operation. There's no one who can look after her, so he has to go away for a few days. Just till she can manage on her own again."

She looked up at Ken, worry on her face.

"He wants us to feed the ducks in the enclosures for him. He says Daniel knows what to do."

"Pity he doesn't do more at home," Ken Murray said. "Finish the jobs here first and then you can go. Ducks won't hurt for waiting a while."

"She can help me shift the pups." Daniel wanted to get away fast. He had a plan, and intended to put it into action, but he would need someone to cover for him.

"If either of you so much as scares one single whisker, I'll feed you to the pike," Ken said. His pups were worth more than gold to him and no young animal must ever be mishandled.

The puppy pen was beside the big enclosure in which rabbits and pheasants lived among the scrubby undergrowth. It was covered with netting to keep out the birds of prey.

The pups watched the birds and rabbits run and jump and play, and learned to ignore them. The older dogs were trained in the pen and woe to any that dared to chase. Blackbird, not yet old enough for breeding, was in training now,

31

and spent hours sitting at Ken's command, while the animals moved around her.

"He's always making me work." Daniel shifted the wheelbarrow, which was in the way. "Never a free minute."

"You're not the only one. I have to collect the eggs and bucket-feed the calves," Anna said. "And bottle-feed the orphan lambs when their mothers die. And the baby pigs, and . . ."

Daniel laughed.

"Slaves, that's what we are. Both of us hard done by."

"Less talk and more work," Ken said, passing them. Anna was welcome so long as she helped and behaved. Ken Murray had no patience with time wasters, and often expected the children to know what he wanted without being shown how to do it.

Jake taught them if they made a mistake, though only Daniel realised that. Anna's father did not allow other children to help on the farm at all. Too much dangerous machinery, he said. Daniel's father accepted their help, but if they made a mistake he was instantly angry, telling them how stupid they were.

Daniel deposited the biggest puppy in the run, and watched as he dashed to the wire, triggered by a black rabbit that appeared suddenly from one of the many pipes that were scattered on the ground in the training pen next door. The rabbits hid in them, played through them, and used them instead of burrows.

The wire checked him. He sat, bright eyed, until three more pups joined him. He forgot the rabbits and nosed his litter mates. Full fed, they were sleepy, and soon the seven were lying in a huddle of black and brown and white, against the wall of the puppy cage, where the sun warmed the heat-reflecting cobbles.

The chores were finished by eleven o'clock. Jennie Murray fed them new-baked shortbread biscuits and home-made lemonade, and sent them off with packs of sandwiches. The men were meeting at lunchtime to discuss the night's shoot. The children were better away. Jennie, like the children, hated the guns.

Ken stored his gun in a cupboard that looked like part of the wall, guarded by a combination lock. The police, inspecting, wished that everyone kept their weapons as securely. Not even Jennie knew where he kept his ammunition.

Daniel's airgun was locked away with them. He was only allowed to use it when his father was with him. He borrowed a gun for the clay-pigeon shooting. Gun drill was part of his life. Never carry a loaded gun. Never point a gun at anyone.

"Only idiots play around with guns," his father said. "Wise men know how to use them, when to use them, and take the greatest care that nobody ever gets hurt by stupidity."

Every gun had to be cleaned before it was put away. Dirty guns could cause accidents.

"Feed the ducks before we eat," Anna said.

Daniel, his mind busy plotting, had to be told twice. If only his plan worked.

Chapter Four

The lake was beyond the old house, across what had once been a terrace and a spacious lawn, parklike, with trees. Anna's great-grandad said the gardens had been designed by Capability Brown, who was one of the best landscape gardeners who ever lived. They were only a memory. It was fifty years since the house had been bombed, and nobody had bothered to keep up with the gardens.

Thistle and nettle and bramble had taken over, and the grounds were a thick maze of dense undergrowth that hid the lawns and beds. Daniel's mother had made a vegetable patch and flower garden near the house, but that was a tiny part of the many acres that had now gone back to the wild.

The maze had become an impenetrable forest. The children hid at the edge of it, but dared not venture inside. The orchard trees were overgrown and gnarled, and the fruit was bitter, as they discovered to their cost when they tried it.

"I've a secret," Anna said, as they walked

past the ballroom. Its windows were bare of glass, and roof was open to the air. "Come and see."

She had to tug at his sleeve.

"Daniel, what on earth is the matter with you? You hardly hear a word I say."

Daniel stared at her. He was so busy thinking about his latest wonderful idea that nothing else seemed to matter. His thoughts both excited and scared him.

"We need to feed the ducks. I was thinking about that," he said, although it wasn't true. He wasn't sure that he wanted to share his idea with Anna.

"They can wait a few minutes." She led the way and Daniel followed, wondering what Anna had hidden.

The door had long gone. It was hidden by a mass of shrubby rhododendron bushes that sneaked their branches into the room itself.

The priesthole was at the far end of the room. Daniel's father had opened it three years before when Anna hid in it and didn't know how to open it from inside. Daniel had found the inner priesthole a year later when exploring the tunnel. He oiled the levers and machinery that opened it. He did not even tell Anna about the second escape route, down worn stone steps and underneath the house into the old kitchen. That led out at the back of a huge cupboard which had probably once stored brooms and brushes and dusters and other cleaning equipment.

The maze of tunnels fascinated him and he had told Anna's great-grandfather about them.

"That house is over seven hundred years old," Nat Colley said. Although he was over ninety he could still drive and help on his good days and his mind was as clear and sharp as it had ever been.

"The whole area is built on rock and there were underground cellars in many houses. When the country became Protestant and Roman Catholics were in danger of death, because the king didn't trust them, the big houses built the priestholes and the priests hid."

Daniel and Anna were fascinated by his stories.

"They were extra clever at Hunter's Keep, as they built a double priesthole. Men searching might find the first. They never dreamed a second was hidden behind it. The passage led to the kitchen so that food could be taken to them without anyone in the big house knowing. There was always danger of treachery."

"Why is there a passage from my room?" Daniel asked.

"They needed more than one, so that there was always an unobserved entrance. Food could be brought to your room, which is just off the old dining room, and then someone could slip away and make sure the priest didn't starve. Sometimes men were in those little cells for years on end. There followed a time when everyone had to change religions. It was death to Protestants then because the queen was a Catholic and *she* didn't trust *Protestants*."

Daniel often thought of the people who had once lived there, of the fear and the secrecy. It must have been very confusing when you lost your life because the new king or queen had a different religion. No one would ever feel safe. Hunter's Keep had been a Cavalier house during the Civil War, and the owner had hidden in his own priesthole, his wife pretending that he had gone to the fight with the king. In fact he had been unable to fight, due to a very lame leg.

Much of the history had been written down by one of the local schoolteachers, who had been enthralled by the story of the big house. Daniel had found it in the reference library.

Anna and Daniel soon found a use for the priesthole, as no one but them ever explored the ruined part of the old house.

They had pets which had to be hidden.

Neither of them was allowed to keep them at home. "Too many animals already," their parents said when asked. "Why do you want more?"

It was difficult to explain that your own rabbit or ferret meant a great deal more than the dogs that boarded, or your uncle's dogs; or that you needed a pet of your own to care for, and not to share. Tish wasn't really Daniel's, as his father bred from her, and took her out with him when there were too many rats. Anna's rabbit had died of old age a few weeks ago.

That had spent its whole life in the ballroom, hidden in a cage behind a stack of planks which had been stored there and forgotten.

Secrets always involved animals. They also involved finding jobs that would pay them enough to earn the food for the animals. Jake knew some of the secrets and helped, and sometimes would come and feed them when the children couldn't get away.

He built several cages, two of them very big, as they had rescued two cats with kittens the year before and found homes for all of them.

They climbed in through one of the windows and walked across the floor. Only the walls reaching to the sky showed this had once been a room. The floorboards were covered with years of rotting leaves, which muffled their tread.

The biggest cage was occupied by a small fluffy bitch with four newborn puppies feeding from her.

Daniel stared at her.

"I found her in our barn," Anna said. "Dad would have sent her to the RSPCA and they'd probably have put her to sleep. He doesn't know I've still got her. I told him she'd run away. She had the pups last night." Daniel looked at her doubtfully.

They had kept rabbits and guinea pigs and ferrets in the priesthole, but never a dog before.

"Suppose she's ill?" Daniel said. "And what will we do with the pups? For that matter, what will we do with her?"

"I hope Jake might have the mother and I've homes for all the pups." Anna was always practical. "I asked everyone in our form."

She stood looking down at the little bitch.

"She's pretty wild. I think she's been thrown out by someone who didn't want pups. She's a Jack Russell cross, probably with collie. I bet the pups' father was a collie. They look much more like collie pups."

The pups were black and white with fluffy fur. They were still very young. There was plenty of room in the cage and they and the bitch would be fine there for the time being. They could come and let her run free each day whenever either of them had time. She'd return to the puppies in her nest.

Daniel, watching her, began to wonder if his idea was so good after all. There were so many snags. Anna would think up even more than he had.

"You said you had an idea." Anna always knew when Daniel was up to something. He hatched new schemes faster than hens laid eggs, she thought.

"I can't save the vixen," he said. "I'm going to save the cubs."

"How?"

"Remember when Tinker was trapped in the old badger diggings at the quarry last year? My dad dug him out?"

Anna nodded. Tinker had raced down the tunnel after a rabbit and been unable to get out again. The men dug for him for three days, and his exploit featured in the daily papers and on the local television news. Daniel went on, his voice eager. "That tunnel leads into the back of the vixen's earth, I'm sure. I can get them out from behind it, when she's away. Jake says she leaves them in the early evening now they are older. I'll be there, hidden, to move the cubs before they find her. I can't stop them killing her on her return. They need proper food now, not just milk, so she is away hunting for longer. They're too young to know fear of people yet."

"It's too dangerous," Anna said. "You don't know how big that tunnel is. You could get trapped, like Tinker."

"It will work." Daniel never allowed any arguments to deter him. "But we can't tell anyone, not even Jake."

"Suppose your father finds them?" Anna knew Ken Murray well. "He'll kill them at once."

"Then he mustn't find them. He never comes near this part of the old house. "

Daniel sounded confident, but he was very far from sure.

He would have to plan, very carefully. Crack-pot, said an inner voice. He knew it was, but he intended to try.

Chapter Five

It was hard to tear themselves away from the bitch and her puppies. Anna put food in the cage, and was rewarded by a low growl and a turned-back lip.

"She doesn't like people," Anna said.

"Probably has good cause. She's been beaten. Look at the marks on her back." Daniel knew a great deal about animals. He had been born into a home where they were all-important. He was always first to spot movement in a field, or the sudden splash of a trout rising from the water.

"We'd better get on and feed the ducks," Daniel said, aware of passing time. He had collected sandwiches, fruit and cake for the two of them before leaving home, so they did not have to hurry back.

Jake was so rarely away that it was odd to walk down to the lake and not see him busying himself with the multitude of chores. Rain speckled the dark water, and overhead the kite roamed the airstreams, watching for movement below.

Daniel, seeing the dead duck at the water's edge, led them along another path towards the little store room where Jake kept the feed. So Blacktip had been here too; and had been interrupted as he fed. Anna pursed her lips, but said nothing. She knew as well as Daniel that the fox had been there the night before.

Daniel vanished and returned with a large old-fashioned key. The store room had once been an air raid shelter, built into the rock. The thick door was proof against marauding animals.

Inside were sacks of feed and rows of pails. Six buckets were already filled.

Anna bent to pick one up.

"Wait!" Daniel said. "Stay just inside the door. You don't know what to do. I do." He often helped Jake feed the ducks, sometimes on his own when the warden had to go away on business.

He walked down to the water's edge, carrying two of the buckets. Suddenly the air was filled with the sound of wings, and deafening bird noise, as ducks and drakes rose from the water, and flew towards him.

They banged at the buckets with their beaks. They perched, covering his head and shoulders and arms. Their wings flailed against his face, their beaks thumped hard against his body.

He tipped the buckets to the ground, scattering the feed, and then ran back to the store.

"Come on, while they're busy, or we'll never get to the pen."

The ground was alive with feeding birds, all busy gobbling.

It was an uphill dash, along a well-trodden path beaten through the bracken. The pen covered several hundred yards, running down a hillside and into the lake. The mesh kept the pike away from the ducklings. The top was covered to keep out the many birds that preyed from the air.

Daniel's father hated them, raiding his woods and taking the tiny chicks. He scared them away with gunfire, and with a scarer that sounded erratically, startling human and bird alike, but apparently having little effect.

Jake enjoyed seeing the hawks, but wished they would hunt elsewhere. There was nothing anyone could do.

"They have to feed," he said. "We kill to feed, too."

"I wish Jake didn't use oil drums for the ducks' shelters at night," Anna said, looking with distaste at the battered containers dotted around the hillside.

"Someone gave them to him for nothing.

They're rainproof and dark, and give shelter to the mother and all her brood." Jake was always bemoaning a lack of money. So, for that matter, was his father. The sale of the pups brought in welcome extras.

But no sane breeder kept his bitches producing pups every six months. Daniel's father let each bitch have three litters, two years apart and then retired them saying they had earned their rest. Puppy rearing was hard work for them.

A duck was dragging dead fronds out of the nearest oil drum, using her beak to ensure that all the old bedding was removed. She waddled over to a pile of cut bracken and took as much as she could carry back to her den.

It was already half full. She trampled it down, turning herself round and round until she had a nest to her liking.

"All the babies are on the water; there's only one duck with them. I wonder how they know which is theirs?" Anna said. Daniel often wondered too.

"I don't know if it's smell . . . do ducks have a sense of smell? I suppose they must do. Or the call they make. Each one sounds a little different if you listen hard." Daniel often sat by the lake. The ducks made so many different sounds: fear, happiness, a crooning lullaby, a call of alarm, a mating call, the call to their babies, a hiss at an intruder.

"Watch," said Daniel. "They'll collect them before coming for the food. They all go into the drums at night, and the duck settles herself in the doorway. Go near and she hisses." Daniel and Jake often spent the sunset hours at the pen. Anna preferred four-legged creatures to those with wings.

Jake had isolated some of the ducks from the drakes, who were all outside the pen. There were ducks outside on the water, too, but their babies were at risk, all the time, from the ravenous pike beneath the surface and the hawks and crows in the air.

One after another, each duck walked down to the lake's edge, and chirruped, a soft odd noise. Little files of downy yellow babies detached themselves. The old grandmother, her duty over as each went back to its own mother, came purposefully up the hill towards the gate.

Daniel eyed them: teal and mallard, pintail and widgeon. Jake had collected more species in the last few weeks.

The big pen, like most places where animals were kept, had two doors with a corridor between. Then, if a duck did get out, there was always the outer door to stop it. It was a firm rule that that door must be shut before the inner door was opened. Escape of any creature was likely to lead to disaster.

He opened the second door, and scattered the food.

There was a flurry of birds, half walking, half flying, even the tiny fluffy mites rushing towards the bounty. Anna stood in the corridor, watching, fascinated. She didn't go further. The ducks were used to Daniel but didn't know her so she might alarm them.

Overhead the clouds darkened and rain lashed down. Anna raced back to the store, leaving Daniel to close the gates. Lightning flickered across the sky and thunder rolled.

They crouched in the doorway, sitting on upturned buckets, watching the lancing light flash again and again across the water.

"One, two, three . . . that was nearly on top of us," Daniel said, counting the interval between the flare and the roar.

"Suppose we're hit by lightning?" Anna said.

Daniel, who was also worried by the severity of the storm, looked out at the tormented sky.

"Maybe if we make ourselves very small the lightning will miss us." He forced a grin and tried to make his voice reassuring, as the thunder growled again. "We won't be. The storm's going away. That was only a tiny rumble, and the lightning's further away, too, right across the lake."

"We'll have to feed the dog before we go home," Anna said. "I left some food in the corner of the ballroom. I hope nothing's eaten it."

The bitch was posing another problem. All very well now, in the holidays, but school began in eight days' time – and what then?

The pups would need more space than they had; the bitch would need exercising. Jake didn't mind them keeping rabbits and ferrets; they didn't need walks. What would he say about a dog? Perhaps he would take her, but she'd have to be trained not to touch the birds. Or kept kennelled – and Jake didn't like penned dogs.

"We'll need a lead and collar for her, and bowls for food," Anna said. She sighed. "She hates people. She could be dangerous." Daniel had tamed young ferrets. They could be vicious unless they were handled sensibly.

"We teach her to like us," he said. "We feed her. We talk to her softly, and reassure her. She'll soon be as friendly as any of our own dogs."

"I'm so used to sensible puppies," Anna said.

Her father bred sheepdogs from his best bitches, and, like Daniel's father, made sure all their pups were handled often by people, and cuddled and petted, before they were sold.

The storm was dying away. The last drops of rain fell through the leaves. The sun, blinking through thinning clouds, shone above the water, laying a golden path.

"A rainbow," Anna said. "Look. A double rainbow, right across the lake." She was entranced.

The coloured arch spanned the sky, flying into the air, glittering, a magical promise of fair weather to come. The brilliant colours shimmered in the sun, shaming the black clouds beyond them. Slowly, it faded, until only a memory was left of its enchantment.

Daniel glanced at his watch. It was later than he realised. He locked the store door and hid the key again, under the biggest log behind the building.

They walked back to Hunter's Keep, taking a short cut that neither of them liked very much, as it led past the broken stone statues that still guarded the avenue. They were enormous and threatening and featured at times in Anna's nightmares. Horrific creatures with damaged limbs, or misshaped noses, eyeless, staring at her from blind sockets.

Daniel made a face at a figure that crouched, its one arm holding a broken bow, a laurel wreath on its faceless head. Years of rain and wind had worn the features away.

The big house brooded, its ruined walls stark against a sky that had changed to a pale blue. They sat for a moment and finished the last of the sandwiches. Anna tidied the wrappings neatly into the bag slung over her shoulder.

They climbed over the sill of an empty window into the ballroom.

The coconut shell filled with dog food was still in the corner where Anna had left it. They took it to the cage, and put it inside. The bitch looked at them, her eyes desperate.

"Suppose it upsets her tummy? She ought to be free to leave her bed," Anna said, worry flaring.

"We'll put her in the inner priesthole. It's sound-proof, so no one can hear the pups there," Daniel said. "There must be air inlets as it never smells musty, like the rest of the old house. People lived in there for weeks."

"Years, sometimes, Grandpa Nat says," he added. He pushed away the thought of being locked away from the world for so long. He was always afraid that one day the mechanism might fail and he would be trapped.

But that didn't prevent him using the passages.

He pressed the nose of the carved cherub at the edge of the outer priesthole. The door swung wide, revealing a room about twelve feet square. Together they lifted the cage and put it inside.

"I'll bring her water later," Daniel said. He undid the latch on the cage door and opened it. The little bitch crouched at the back, glaring at them. "She'll eat when we're gone and come out when she feels it's safe to do so. I can clean up after her. There's lots of room."

"It's so dark," Anna said. "Imagine being shut in here for days on end, while soldiers hunted for you."

"They'd have lamps. And people to bring them food. It's better than being dead." There were more practical things to consider. "If your father takes her to the rescue people she might well be put to sleep at the end of a week or so. They're overcrowded."

Daniel closed the outer door. It slid silently into place at a touch of the moulding.

"I don't like leaving her in there, all the same," Anna said.

"She has her pups. And she's safe. She'll probably be happier there than in the barn, where there are rats and cats, and people who terrify her." Daniel sounded confident.

Anna glanced at her watch.

"Hey, I'm off, or I'll be in big trouble. It's time the calves were fed. See you." She was away, running through the gathering dusk, her long legs in their blue jeans covering the ground in immense strides. Anna hoped to run for her county.

Daniel watched until she was out of sight. He'd use the tunnel and be back in his room, coming from the inside of the house and not outside and then maybe his parents wouldn't be so mad at him. He was late, too. Too late to feed the pups, and that was his job. His father would be angry.

He opened the priesthole again. The bitch hadn't moved. The light was dim, but he could see her, lying against the back of the cage, apparently ignoring the door that led to freedom. She watched as he closed the door. He knew the way across the room, and felt for the knob that would open the tunnel entrance. A moment later he was inside, taking the torch off the little shelf, knowing the routine so well he barely needed light.

He often wondered who had made this underground system that led from cellar to store room to still room to the library, where there was a peephole in the wall, with others in the ballroom and the old dining and drawing rooms.

Who hid in them? Who watched?

He marked each fork in the passage with painted arrows. Nobody but he ever came here now, he was sure.

Along the stone floor, past the library and the picture gallery. They said that was haunted. He held his breath, always afraid that some apparition might spring on him, but the only creatures he ever met were bats.

The air was thick with them at night, and the place smelled musty, the floor littered with droppings. By day they hung in clusters and did not move. They flew out through openings so tiny that Daniel was only aware of them by the breath of wind that came through them. They came out in the fountain, and he suspected there were other openings that he had never found.

They swooped through the air above the pheasant pens, hunting for insects. Daniel was always afraid his father would try to find out where they hid by day, and stumble on the tunnel, but they did no harm to the game birds, and Ken Murray was unworried by their presence.

Back in his room, he closed the tunnel

entrance. He looked at the mantelpiece. No one would think the carved swans held secrets. He washed hastily, and slipped along the corridor to the kitchen.

They lived in the old servants' quarters; room for an army, Daniel sometimes thought. His mother complained about the amount of cleaning. No wonder the Lord and his family wanted to live in a modern house.

"You're late," Jennie said, spooning curry and rice on to his plate. She had cooked the remains of one of last year's frozen pheasants. Keeper's perks, his dad said. They ate like kings, his mother said. Pheasant, grouse, partridge, quail, sometimes salmon. Trout, which he and his father caught in the little stream. Sometimes a rabbit or a hare.

"Sheltered from the storm," Daniel said by way of explanation. He was busy, and didn't want to answer. He had not realised how hungry he was.

"Don't talk with your mouth full." He sensed his mother had her mind on something else. He swallowed. It was a token statement. Conversation without saying anything that mattered.

"You asked me. Where's Dad?"

"Out."

"After the foxes?"

"Yes." His mother looked at him unhappily. "I don't like it, either, love, but there are far too many. They have to be kept down somehow and now hunting's stopped, there're only the guns. Don't annoy your father, please."

I'm too late, Daniel thought miserably. The cubs will all be dead. He had completely miscalculated. Why did people never do what you thought they would?

"Why did they go so early?"

"The farm over at Penside lost all its laying birds last night. They were afraid if they waited till she came home they'd miss her. No one knows the exact timing of her movements and anything might change that. A hooting car, or a badger in the area, as he might kill the cubs. They want her to bolt so that they can catch her in the open and shoot her. A quick death. There's a back way into that particular den, so they can send the dogs in there. She'll come out in the quarry, trying to escape rather than fight. She'll chase the cubs out, and hope they can all survive. They'll catch the whole family that way."

"How do you know so much?"

"Jake tells me. I don't tell your father."

He had lost his appetite. He ate the rest of his meal with difficulty, forcing himself to swallow, knowing his mother would be upset if he left the food she had spent so long cooking, and would take his temperature and fuss.

"I've choir practice tonight. You'll be all right on your own?"

She asked him every week, and every week he said yes. Sometimes he joined Jake, sometimes he went round the pheasant pens with his father, or patrolled the woods with him, looking for snares, which were sometimes set by poachers and were a danger to cats and dogs as well as the rabbits they were intended to catch. Often he walked in the woods by himself. He saw people there, and vans and cars, and noted the numbers and told them to Jake, who told the police.

"Be careful," Jake said. "If you hear anyone, lie down. Bury your face in the ground, so they don't see the white or the flash of your eyes and put your hands underneath you."

Daniel always lay flat, careful not to disturb the branches, or tread on fallen twigs that made a doomsday crack that even the most inexperienced townsman could detect.

What kind of people were they, out at night? Sometimes they had packages which were transferred from van to car, or vice versa. He never knew what they did, or why they were there. He was never close enough to overhear, and he took great care never to be seen. Once he had climbed a tree and perched there uncomfortably for over two hours, until the van and car drove away.

He was glad he stayed as, when all was quiet again, two badgers walked down the ride, their white stripes gleaming in the moonlight. He watched them sit and scratch and then play tag with one another. Not cubs, yet not grown, full of delight in being alive.

"Never tell anyone about them," Jake said.

The people he feared most were the terrier men with their leather jackets, sideburns, dark caps and busy little dogs, out after the badgers. Then he used the tunnel to race home and ring Jake, who operated a badger-watch scheme.

He needed to feed the bitch daily. No use relying on the others. Anna had her own chores on the farm, as he did with his father's dogs, and with the pheasant feeding. He lived in Hunter's Keep; she had a long walk to reach them, and certainly couldn't manage to do so before school.

Other children living in towns often didn't know they were born, he thought.

Their new commitment needed a name. Maybe they ought to take her to the rescue kennels, but if nobody wanted her she would be put to sleep in another seven days – and how could he allow that?

He fetched a water carrier, and looked for a basin that his mother would not miss. He chose a rough old bowl with a blue design that had been at the back of the cupboard for years.

He filled his pocket with dog biscuits, and set off along the tunnel. Afterwards, he would go down to the quarry and see if they had killed the vixen and her cubs.

He thought of them, playing in the moonshine, unaware that they had so little time to live. He hated people, who always put their own needs first.

Chapter Six

Blacktip had been hunting busily ever since the cubs were born. Food was scarce, as myxomatosis had caused death among the rabbits. Poachers shot the hares, and he was forced to hunt among the farm chickens and the pheasant coppices.

His territory stretched from the edge of the moors, over the farmland that fringed Hunter's Keep, across the woods that belonged to the old mansion, and beyond the kennels on the other side towards the wildlife sanctuary.

He avoided the hen houses, and looked for the stray bird that had failed to return to roost at night, or settled under a hedge to rear her chicks, away from the farm where her eggs were taken from her.

He knew that at times there was food left for the cats on the farm, as they lived out of doors, to keep the rats away from the stored animal food. Nobody realised that Blacktip also helped to kill the rats. He also took the food from the bowls, and left hungry cats that turned with even more enthusiasm to their night-time hunts.

Twice he avoided the guns. Once he sped into the thick cover of thorny bramble, as Ken Murray saw him and missed his target. He hid in the base of an old tree. The second time he was close to an old mine working, and fled down the tunnel to crouch behind the tumble of rock that had almost closed it.

That time it was Sly Cooper, who poached relentlessly, and was rarely caught. He hoped to gain approval instead of condemnation, by removing one of the area's known enemies. There was room for Blacktip to creep, and Sly's lurcher was at home with her new litter of pups. Had she been there, there might have been a different end to the story.

The vixen was exhausted. The five cubs drained her energy and she herself was unable to hunt far afield. She was wary, knowing there was danger for her and her babies. Instinct kept her nose sniffing the air. Her ears moved constantly, forwards and backwards, listening for the rumours brought to her on the wind. Her body was tense, aware of the vibration in the ground that told of heavy creatures moving.

It might be horses, as the riders took the way through the woods. It might be deer, alerted by their own sentries, who gave a quick stamp and snort at any sign of danger, so that they all fled together. It might be the two-legged giants who moved with such lack of caution that they crashed through bushes, thundered over the ground and cracked the dead twigs that littered the paths. They held the sticks that spoke and brought swift death. She had seen her own father tumble to the guns.

Beware two legs, her actions told the cubs. They mean danger. They are more wicked and more cunning than hawk or snake or weasel and can kill from many yards away. She tried to convey her terror of men to her babies, so that they would become as wise and canny as she herself.

The cubs were growing and were too adventurous. The biggest strayed often, entranced by the wind on the water in the quarry pit far below. Death waited for them everywhere. Death from the hunting hawk. Death from the soaring kite. Death from the long drop to the killing water. She taught them to run and hide when the great shadows of the giant birds fled over the grass, and sometimes they hid too from the shapes of passing clouds, unable to tell the difference.

"Freeze," she told them, over and over again, but little cubs rarely listened and she had to reinforce her commands with a busy slapping paw and nips and bites.

The three little females were the most biddable, and the most affectionate, curling up against her, nuzzling her, whimpering to her softly. They were always the first to greet her when she came home from a foraging expedition. They ran to her, lifting their heads to her face, eager for her licking tongue to reassure them, and hungry for the food she brought them.

Each time she counted heads. One, two, three, four, five. Though she had no words she had a sense of number, and knew at once if one was missing.

Little Blacktip was adventurous and on one occasion began to explore. The vixen never forgot that she had come home and found him missing. Movement alerted him, below the lip of the quarry, on the steep sloping path that led to the water that had collected over the years. He crept downwards, entranced. There was so much to see. A beetle, black with a brilliant blue edge to its body. He teased it with a tentative paw and then crunched it, savouring his first kill. He longed now for more than his mother's milk and chewed at the bones she left.

There was a smell on the wind that drew him downwards. There were birds below him, diving and darting, skimming in the air and flashing over the water, and as he crept on, the smell of them was stronger, calling him.

Age-old instincts told him here was food, but he had no idea how he would catch that food, nor did he know that the birds were airborne, though below him. A heron brooded at the edge of the water, watching for fish.

Bright flowers starred the grass. He sniffed at one as it bowed in the wind and the pollen made him sneeze.

He did not see his mother approach. She snarled at him, angry, because he had risked his life. She took him by the scruff of his neck and carried him, squealing his indignation, up the path. She threw him down on the ledge, safely among the other cubs, and told him, in deep growls, that this must never happen again.

He cowered in front of her, shocked by her anger. He had never seen her so furious. Her own fear for his safety made her snarl at him again and he crouched and whimpered at her. Relenting, she put her paw on him, washed him with swift licks, and then nuzzled him against her so that he fed. He snuffled himself to sleep, still making small unhappy sounds, as he dreamed again of his venture into the wild unknown and his mother's pounce on him from above. She rested her head on his back and cuddled him close between her paws and he settled, the dream banished by her comforting presence.

The cubs needed meat. The vixen had no choice but to leave them for longer and longer periods, hoping that the bright moonlight would not entice them into danger.

Soon it would be time to teach them hunting, to teach them the wild ways, the paths that were only known to fox and badger and deer. Teach them the secrets of the hollow trees, of the tunnels among bracken and thorn that led to safety.

Cubs that disobeyed or refused to learn were dead cubs.

Hide, little ones, hide. The two-legged giants walk here. Listen to the thump and thunder of their huge feet. Listen to the bellow of their great voices and the roar of their laughter. Watch for the burning they leave behind them, from the strange little objects they put in their mouths to the fires they light to cook their food.

Above all avoid their children with their screaming voices. They never see where they run and their great hooves could crush you. Though they are small they thump over the ground, and their hands hurt.

The vixen had once been caught by humans and handled by children who crushed her and bruised her and grabbed her, holding her too tightly. They lifted her in the air, so that the ground was far away, and then they put her down so hard that she hurt herself each time. They breathed at her and screamed at her. She could not bear their smell. She escaped to safety, racing off one day through a gap in the garden fence that no one knew existed.

She had never forgotten her brief unhappy spell among the two-legged giants.

They never think of any other creatures but themselves and relate all the world to them. They break and soil everything they touch. They leave danger behind them: broken glass that cuts, so that you bleed to death; cans half full of food that entice you to put your heads inside and then you are trapped.

Their food will poison you so that you die. They throw it away, half eaten and it goes bad. It is bad for us. Their dogs chase and kill.

There was so much to teach them that she knew, yet could not convey. They could only learn, as she had, by seeing other creatures suffer and die, some killed by hawks, others killed by the debris left behind by the two legs.

Hide. Keep away. Keep safe. Only the wise

ones live. Like your father, who is older than most foxes, and has more cunning in the tip of his tail than most.

She could not talk to them, but she could convey feelings; convey her fear when Sly Cooper and his four sons walked with their guns in the woods. Sly was clever, and could call the pheasants from their roosts with a soft whistle and then kill them with his catapult.

At times he put down grain soaked in whisky, so that the birds were dizzy and sick and he and his sons could take them at will.

The vixen tasted the grain and felt ill for hours, snarling at her cubs when they tried to feed.

As the days passed the cubs grew. They played and rolled and teased and twisted. The biggest of them, the little male with the black tip tail that characterised his father, was ever more impatient to see the world beyond the den.

There were enticing smells in the air. He learned to know the throat-catching, acrid smell of humans – that he hated. It spoke of danger; it spoke of fear. He knew the smell of mouse and rat, as they were the offerings that Blacktip often brought. He loved feathers, and when the birds were eaten, played with the long tail feathers of the pheasants, teasing them and tossing them.

It was fun when the wind blew and lifted them on its unseen currents, and he could chase them as if they were alive. His bright eyes grew even more brilliant, his pricked ears moved forwards and backwards in excitement, and he bumbled on small unsteady paws, practising being grown, pretending he was as mighty a hunter as his father. He pounced, kittenlike, and then tossed the feather into the air so that the game could begin again, as fresh as if it had never happened before.

Life was all excitement.

He growled at his brother and sisters if they dared to interfere with his play. He seldom joined in their romps as they rolled and bit and fought, pretending to be angry with one another. The games might end in a chase along the quarry ledge, the vixen watching them, ready to leap in and drag back any baby that ventured too near the drop.

Or it might end in a small tumble of furry bodies curled up close against one another, sleeping. Little Blacktip joined them when he slept, when dawn brought birdsong and the dangerous, all-revealing light. He preferred to play alone. He it was that ruled them all; he ran in, snarling, if the games grew too fierce and his mother was away.

The vixen was hunting the night the weasel came. The lithe beast was small and he was hungry, and he knew where the cubs hid. Little Blacktip saw the flicker of the brown body in the grass. He yickered sharply as his mother would have done, and the cubs ran to shelter, hiding in the crack at the back of the den.

The weasel lifted his head. He began to dance, and the cubs watched, intrigued, as he twisted and turned; he somersaulted, chasing his tail; he spun in giddy circles, so that the tiny animals, watching, were intrigued and forgot danger.

They crept to the opening of the den, fascinated by this whirling animal that performed for them, that leaped in the air, that moved so fast he was a blur of fur, weaving in and out of the long grass, now invisible, now suddenly close to them.

He paused, and crouched to spring.

Blacktip raced down the quarry path, having seen the dance from above. He caught the weasel with an angry paw, so that it twisted, off balance, and fell over the ledge, towards the water. It caught in the bushes below and crawled, sore from the blow and bruised from the fall, and vanished, still hungry.

Blacktip scolded the cubs.

Then, relenting, he indulged in a rare game with them, so that they climbed over him and chased his tail. The vixen, returning, lay to watch. She had caught nothing and was hungry. Blacktip had brought a pheasant with him, and discarded it when he saw the weasel. She found it and ate. It was dark, the moon hiding behind gauzy clouds, and there was little wind. Nothing to warn them. The wind could be a friend, bringing news, or an enemy, cloaking the scent that it took away from them.

The days and nights passed. They played and squabbled and slept, and each new day brought fresh excitement. They did not know their wonderful way of life was to end, suddenly.

None of them saw or heard the men who crept, and watched, and then shot. Little Blacktip was outside when the dogs came in. He hid, in the shadow of two enormous boulders, and the wind blew the dogs' scent to him, but not his to the dogs. He lay, trembling with terror, and saw his mother and his father die, saw the dogs that ran down the quarry edge to take his brother and his sisters. He stumbled into the lair, away from danger, knowing only terror. The dogs were too busy with their captives to scent him or see him.

He lay in the darkness, while the men took

the bodies of his parents and brother and sisters away, and did not understand what had happened. He only knew he was alone, and that he was too small to hunt for himself, or to travel the quarry path that his parents took when they went out to hunt.

He crept into the cranny at the back of the den, afraid to move. He longed for his mother to come, to nose him, and to lie for him to feed. He longed for his father to come, to play with him, to wave his bushy tail, teasing. He longed for his sisters to curl up against him, for his brother to try and take his feather from him.

He whimpered forlornly in the empty lair. He whimpered for his mother, and because of the strange smells that were all around him: scent of dog and smell of man and the appalling aftermath of sudden death. He whimpered when clouds cleared and the moon shone high and full. There was no one to hear.

Chapter Seven

There was so much to plan and it was all difficult. Daniel wished that he had brothers and sisters. If only Anna lived nearer, but the farm was four fields away from his home. Both children used the fields as short cuts, but were not supposed to do so.

It was an adventure to creep round the sides of them against the hedges and climb the gates. Ramblers tended to open them; picnickers tended to think that grass fields were devoid of crops, when the hay was growing. So now they were padlocked. Straying animals were costly, especially if they were killed on the road or found by the police and the owner heavily fined.

A holidaymaker four years ago had let a ram out of a field. It attacked a woman and broke her leg. She sued the farmer. His prize-winning thousand-guinea ram was put down, and he had to pay a fortune in compensation. The ram was insured against illness, theft and death, but not against injuring anyone.

Even if there were no accidents, hours were

wasted in herding them back. Farmers never had time to spare. Today, with few men to help them, they lived life at the gallop.

Daniel sat and thought. Now that the time had come to act he didn't want to venture alone, but he had no choice. There was no way of rousing Anna once she was in bed. The farmhouse had gravel paths around it, and gravel scrunched.

He had to find food for the bitch. No use asking his parents. No use telling Anna's parents. They all said firmly no more dogs, unless they were working sheepdogs, bred on the farm, or working gundogs, bred in the kennels.

She would be removed at once, and the pups put to sleep, and maybe she too would die. Life had too many problems. She was more than half starved, so really needed to be fed little and often and how on earth did he do that when he was at school?

Maybe if he fed her at 6 a.m. and again at 8.30. Then he could cycle home at lunch time. It wouldn't leave much time, but it could just be done. He would have to go the long way, or his parents would see him. No use asking the others. None of them had bikes.

He could then feed at 5 p.m. and at 10 p.m.

For once he would be really efficient and put out the food for the pups at night, and store it in the refrigerator. It didn't need to be refrigerated but he couldn't think of any other place that his father would miss seeing.

If Daniel took a tablespoonful from each, his father wouldn't notice. He needed something to store it in.

His lunch box. He filled it, hoping that the pups wouldn't miss the tiny amount he took from each dish.

His mother, returning home at half past ten, opened the refrigerator. She needed milk for her bedtime drink. She looked at the puppy plates, neatly stacked with the rings she used in cooking.

"That should save a lot of time in the morning," she commented, knowing why they were hidden there. She smiled at Daniel, who promptly felt as if she could read his mind and know he was hiding a guilty secret from her.

Several, in fact. There was the hidden bitch, and the stolen food, as well as his plan that would, if found out, bring nothing but trouble on him.

"Bed, young man, or you won't be up in time even to take them out of the fridge." She ruffled his hair, instead of kissing him goodnight.

Daniel wasn't sure which he hated most.

He waited until midnight. He read his book by torchlight, under the covers, so that no glint would show. His mother rarely came into his room after he went to bed, but there was always the chance she might look for one of his shirts, in need of a button, or check that he was asleep.

The cuckoo clock in the kitchen sang its mad little song.

His father was not yet back. He often patrolled the woods at night, as that was when the poachers came. His mother had gone to bed at eleven and was asleep.

He had learned to move without making any sound. Barefoot, he padded across the room and pressed the knob that controlled the switch. The door swung open, revealing the darkness below.

He put on the black jersey that his mother had given him for the school jumble sale. He kept it hidden inside the secret passage. Dark jeans and dark trainers completed his outfit.

The torch flashed over the rough floor. Daniel always felt a tremor of fear as he walked along the passages, which had been unknown to anyone but him for who knows how many years.

The woods hid poachers; not the old men his grandfather knew, but a wild modern breed, without pity or conscience, who came in gangs, armed with guns, and were as little likely to care about shooting a man or a boy who saw them as shooting an animal. .

Suppose they knew of the passages under the house? It had been famous in its time and written about in magazines. The lost tunnels had been mentioned, though the writers did not know that they still existed. Criminals were always looking for safe hiding places to stow their loot, and this would be ideal.

Anyone running through the woods and stumbling into the fountain might find the hidden entrance by accident, as he had.

Here in the tunnel was absolute dark, and though he used his torch at intervals, there was always the heartstopping fear that others might know the hidden ways and use the tunnels to hide stolen booty.

It was a fear he would never confess to anyone. He never confessed either to pain, as his father had no time for moaners. Ken Murray dismissed any ache as imaginary nonsense. He never even seemed to have a cold, and the only time Daniel had known him stay off work was the night that a poacher shot him in the arm. The man was in jail. One of Ken's triumphs, and he boasted of his arrest of the villain in spite of a useless and bleeding arm.

Daniel wished he could stop his busy mind from thinking. His thoughts were unpleasant company.

There was a rustle as something moved in the dark, and a sudden eerie moan, distorted by the rocky walls. There was another rustle, and then the musky sharp smell that he knew well. Only bats. He relaxed. Had there been people in the tunnel they would have gone. Would ghosts drive them away?

For some reason he felt more uneasy than usual. The passages always filled him with dread, but usually he laughed at his imaginings, and conquered them. Tonight it was worse than he had ever known it, and he almost turned back to go to his bed.

The thought of the foxcubs prevented him from that. Maybe the men hadn't found the vixen yet. Maybe he could confront them and persuade them to leave her alone. He knew even as he thought that that if he was seen there would be major trouble. His father would be furious with a son wandering alone at midnight.

He wished his torch did not cast such odd shadows. The shadows seemed to move and breathe. His own shadow shifted unnervingly and at times was almost unrecognisable.

He had his lunch box under his arm. The

pups dry, all-purpose diet wouldn't go off. He could hide it in the priest-hole. He would have to tell his mother he had left the box at school at the end of term, and hope she had not noticed that it had been in his room.

He would have to make a list of the lies he told so that he told the same one every time.

The passage from his room led upwards, and branched to slope steeply towards the first floor of the old house. Then he came to a flight of steps, leading down again to the ground floor and the priesthole. One, two, three . . . Daniel had a sudden horrifying memory of a story he had once read, about a woman who had been told that the church she was visiting connected directly with hell.

She laughed.

For all that she counted as she descended the stairs to the crypt. One hundred and ten steps. The story ended with her going down, terrified, and counting . . . one thousand and one, one thousand and two, one thousand and three. Maybe not those numbers, but she had gone well below the grounds of the church and was still descending.

The story had haunted his dreams for weeks.

Suppose one night there were flights of stairs he had never seen before, leading down into unimaginable horrors. The trouble was that he could imagine the horrors only too easily. It must be nice to have no imagination. Who said that a coward died a thousand deaths, a fool but one? Or was it a brave man only one?

There were sixteen steps. He counted them, and felt outwards for the rocky floor, afraid of missing the last step and falling. There was a spyhole here which opened into his parents' room. It was hidden behind a picture, but a line of light might show if he used his torch.

Were there ghosts here, remembering old deeds long forgotten? Had priests hidden here, afraid of capture and death? Had Roundheads attacked here as the family had been King Charles' men? They had lost their home to Cromwell, but had it restored when the king came back to the throne.

A bat squeaked and Daniel froze, until he recognised the sound. He put out his hand as he had switched off the torch. Rough rocky walls, damp to the touch.

He swallowed.

Was that a groan in the distance?

Suppose someone took refuge here who was injured and he had to go for help and reveal his secret? The noise came again and he drew a quick breath of relief. It was a puppy, seeking its mother, maybe strayed across the nest away from her warmth.

The tunnel distorted the sound, magnified it and echoed it in eerie overtones.

It must be wonderful to be Jake and grown-up and afraid of nothing, instead of being trapped in a twelve-year-old body with fears that Daniel sometimes thought really belonged to a five-year-old. Nobody would ever be allowed to guess that he was scared.

Another few steps, holding his breath, hoping he did not suddenly touch someone unknown in the dark. It was safe to put his torch on again. He would be glad when he reached the priest-hole. It seemed even further away than usual.

Beyond it was freedom, up the steps to the priesthole, and then to the woods outside where he could lose himself easily. He knew every inch of them, knew where to creep and hide when vans passed down the rides, or his father patrolled, or the police car drove by.

Here, there was nowhere to run if intruders caught him.

Maybe they would be looking for treasure, not hiding it. There often was treasure hidden in old passages in these ancient buildings. Suppose they tortured him to make him tell where it was hidden? He had a longing for bright lights that came at the flick of a switch, for company.

He froze against the wall. There were strange sounds where there should be silence. Eerie movements, and a sudden thump. Everything echoed down here, and noises were distorted.

He forced himself on. He had to conquer his fears. His father had no respect at all for a son who was afraid of shadows and of creatures conjured up by his own lively imagination.

Only a few more yards and he would be out in the open and able to see all around him.

Chapter Eight

The noises ceased. Daniel was aware that his heart was thumping fast, and that his hands were wet with sweat. It was now much further back along the passage than it was to go forward.

He took a deep breath and nerved himself and went on. He reached the priesthole at last and as he opened the door he realised, with relief, that what he had heard had only been the soft murmurs of feeding puppies, and a thump as one of them had rolled off his mother and landed on the wooden floor.

There was a rustle of movement in the straw that Anna had brought from the farm. This was followed by a small squeak as one of the pups lost the teat. Daniel put the torch on the floor, the light shining away from the little family.

The bitch lifted her head, and, recognising him, settled herself again. She did not greet people with enthusiasm. She had not yet learned to trust. He scattered a handful of food on the floor of her cage. She made no move towards it or him, and he left her, hoping she would eat when he had gone.

He filled the big blue bowl with water and slipped that into the cage. He spoke to her softly.

"Good girl. Eat up. I'll be back in the morning."

She gave a half-hearted wave of her tail, her eyes watching him, anxious, afraid he might harm her. He sighed as he left her.

The door of the priesthole closed behind him, sliding on silken hinges. Once it had squeaked, but he now kept it oiled. Across the leaf-strewn floor, through the window and out into the night.

The long soft moan was repeated and he grinned. Only two owls, calling to one another as they hunted.

There was only the ghost of a faint full moon, now masked by hazy cloud, a glint of light, high in the sky. The cloud was shifting, blown by a wind that rustled the leaves and stirred the grass and made eerie heartstopping noises. If it cleared that would bring light, but also danger as he could be seen as easily as he could see. Light could also be an enemy. Maybe the clouds were gathering and would help him stay hidden.

Orion shone bright. No time for stargazing tonight. He ran softly down the ride, the turf mossy under his feet.

His worst fears were realised. He heard the sound of heavy footsteps. More than one man. He threw himself flat, a bramble scraping his face. He held his breath, the earth choking him, making him want to cough. Nettles stung his right hand. He knew it was the hunting party with their guns, his father leading them. They paused where the trails separated. They were so close that he could see his father's boot.

"Four cubs and the vixen. A good night's work," a voice said. A Jack Russell nosed Daniel's cheek. Daniel held his breath. Would the dog bark? It was Rip, who belonged to one of the farmers. Daniel searched in his pockets and found two liquorice allsorts.

"Shhh," he said, as he gave them to the dog. It took them eagerly and licked his face.

"Rip!" The voice was sharp. Disobedience would be punished. Rip raced off and Daniel relaxed. The other dogs would not leave their masters' heels. Hunting on their own was a major crime.

Four cubs. There had been five. They'd missed one. He couldn't save the rest, but perhaps this one was unharmed. The men were chatting. Would they never go?

It seemed hours before they moved on.

Daniel was about to stand when he heard a rustle in the bushes. Something large was there. Another man, hidden, watching for poachers? The leaves parted, and he found himself staring at the striped head of a boar badger, which snuffled angrily and turned aside, startled to find a human lying in its path.

There were setts beyond the quarry, but he had thought they were now occupied by foxes. He had not seen a badger in this part of the woods before. They must live close to the vixen. He thought of the empty den, and wished that animals and people could co-exist. Why did they have to kill her?

The moon vanished and a thin rain began to fall. Daniel kept beneath the trees, freezing against a trunk whenever he heard a noise, but most of the sounds were those of small animals moving in the undergrowth. His frequent late explorations had given him keen night sight, and he stopped once when a bush moved suddenly.

A roe deer stared at him, eyes wide and alarmed, then gave a short explosive bark and jumped away. Beyond it two rabbits sat up on their haunches, and then they too were gone, bounding fast into the bushes, away from danger.

Every time any creature moved, Daniel thought his heart would race itself so fast that it broke. Did hearts over-rev like engines? He was sure his did.

Why come when you're so scared? he asked himself. He knew the answer to that. He had to prove to himself he was as brave as his father; and had never to let his father know of his fears. No one else must ever know. He didn't want his father to catch him when out, but he felt that his excursions proved he was brave.

Maybe if his father did discover him he would think so too. If only he could tell him; could share these night-time walks, could show him the creatures that he and Jake watched, and know that he and his father shared the same feelings. Only he knew that they did not.

His father admired all the tough qualities that some boys at school possessed, but that Daniel did not. Like Mark who came clay-pigeon shooting with his father and hit the target every time, who was in the school first eleven for cricket, in the rugby team, and who seemed afraid of nothing.

Daniel loved poetry and wrote it, though he

kept his poems well hidden. Ken Murray had little time for books. His work was his passion, his guns his treasures, and he could not understand anyone who wanted to sit and think or read when life was beckoning and there were so many outdoor pursuits.

His father knew where every creature laired, where the wild birds nested, where the rats came up to steal. He could see where the pheasants had parted the grass, could stop, knowing a partridge was within an inch of his toe, and yet he did not share Daniel's wonder or Jake's delight.

An owl hooted again, the sound long and eerie. A distant voice echoed it. The rain made the path slippery. Long grass soaked the legs of his jeans and he wished he had been able to wear wellingtons, but no one could walk quietly in those.

At the edge of the quarry he crouched, listening. The entrance to the tunnel the men had made to dig out the terrier was black against the lighter stone. He slipped inside. The entrance was big enough for him to stoop, but it soon narrowed.

He lay flat, listening. Night sounds were always alarming because they were made by invisible creatures. There was a sudden huff from lower down the quarry. What was foraging there?

Badger?

Or was there an adult fox left alive? The cubs were far too small to make so much noise. Then the rustling ceased, and it was silent except for the faraway rumble of a passing train.

Somewhere beyond him he heard the soft keening whimper of an abandoned cub.

It was alive!

He crept forward, afraid to shine the torch. It would startle the baby, and then it might run away, out into the night, and over the edge of the ground that lipped the entrance. Daniel did not know how much of the tunnel there was between him and the back of the den.

There was no watchful mother to alert her baby to danger and bring it back to safety, carrying it in her jaws. To hiss to it so that it froze, flattened against the ground, not a movement betraying its presence, while the roving hawk soared overhead, darkening them with its shadow, and then, seeing nothing below, flew off.

He crawled again, feeling the earth too close around him, smelling the dank musty overpowering reek of fox. It was hard to go on.

Suppose the tunnel collapsed. Nobody knew he was here. They would hunt and hunt in vain and he would die there, smothered, and maybe not be found until another terrier was trapped.

Or would they send out the police dogs? Would the dogs find his trail and scent him, and discover only a corpse? Would his father be sorry that he had lost his son? Would he think him brave for venturing out alone, or be angry at what he considered sheer stupidity?

He was tired. He longed for bed, for sleep, but he had to find the cub. And then what?

The forlorn sound was nearer. He stretched out his arm. Earth. Rock. A gap. There was a crack in the wall, no more. The tunnel had ended. He reached into the crack and encountered a small furry body. Sharp teeth sank into his hand. That was going to be hard to explain. One of the puppies would have to take the blame.

And if his father saw the bite, he'd be punished for teasing it, as happy pups didn't bite people. Not his father's pups. Maybe that was a bad idea. Perhaps he'd have a better one on the way home. He had an overwhelming longing for Jake, who would know what to do. Who always knew what to do.

Another twelve years and he'd be as old as

Jake. Lucky Jake, to have left school and be out in the exciting adult world and not have any worries. Well, not real ones. He was big enough to overcome all of them.

The tiny animal clung to the hand. Daniel brought it close to him, and detached the sharp teeth. He sucked at the bite. It was painful. How old was this cub? Was it yet weaned? He had a piece of cheese in his pocket, and he held it out to the small mouth. The cub took it eagerly.

He tucked it against him and turned to crawl out. Headlights scythed the ground outside, and he heard the sound of an engine that was instantly silenced. The lights went out.

Who was out there now? He had a vision of a gang of men, intent on sharing out the proceeds of a bank robbery, or maybe a drug haul. If they found him they might kill him. The newspapers were full of stories of terrible people and terrible deeds. Or they'd hold him hostage maybe, tied up, chained, or bound and gagged. Nothing would drag the knowledge from him.

He grinned, knowing his thoughts were daft. It would be difficult to give anything away as he didn't know what knowledge he had that would interest anyone, except perhaps that of the secret tunnels. And that was going to stay secret.

He froze against the ground, making himself

small, making himself invisible, praying the cub wouldn't whimper.

"Quiet tonight," said a voice. It was accompanied by an odd mutter, that Daniel suddenly realised was a personal radio. He was trapped by a police car. That was nearly as bad as being caught by a gang of crooks. Well, they wouldn't torture him or take him hostage.

They would take him home and wake his father. If he were in and not still out in the woods himself. And if his father knew Daniel had been out at night, there would be a raging and a roaring, and Daniel hated that.

So did his mother. Both of them crept around white-faced and silent after one of his dad's royal rages, as his mum called them. Even the dogs were subdued and took care to obey the second they were given a command.

"Don't provoke him, Daniel, please," she'd beg. "He doesn't mean it when he yells, but so many things upset him."

Daniel sighed. He often thought his father seemed only to relate every creature to the needs of the pheasants he reared so well, and to be unable to understand either his wife or his son, though his mother never complained.

Ken's other passion was training the dogs and competing in the gundog trials. He had to win, and if he didn't then they all suffered for the next few weeks. He represented England in the International. They always prayed he would do well enough to be part of the team. The days of competition were nail-biting days.

Grandfather Murray had been a gamekeeper too, and won many events. Grandfather Paterson, who had worked as a signalman on the railway, disapproved.

"It's not the winning, boy. That doesn't count. It's being in a team. And it's always more fun to travel than to arrive."

That was Tasha's Grandad, named after his standard poodle, to distinguish him from Grandad Murray, who was Thor's Grandad, after his bull terrier. Tasha's Grandad was a very quiet man. Daniel loved his visits. Thor's Grandad was as fierce as his son and even easier to rouse to anger. Luckily his wife could calm him quickly, but if he came alone both Daniel and his mother dreaded his visits.

Especially if his father and his grandfather had a roaring match, as they seldom agreed on anything.

"Why does Dad have to arrange all the shoots?" Daniel had asked when he was very small. He thought of that now, trying to ease a cramped leg and an arm with pins and needles.

"The old Lord has a syndicate for the shoots," his mother said. "The syndicate pay well, and he can then afford to pay your father a big bonus, and some of the men tip handsomely. We need the money. Life's so expensive these days."

The policemen showed no sign of moving. One of them was sitting on the ground, and Daniel heard a rustle. They were eating sandwiches.

"Coffee?" asked a voice.

"Sure. Not much sign of life here tonight," replied the other man.

Daniel had an overwhelming desire to sneeze. He pressed his finger hard under his nose, though that wasn't always guaranteed to work. This time it did and he drew a soft breath thankfully. The tiny dial on his luminous watch said 2 a.m. No time for a boy to be out on his own. The last thing he needed was to be discovered.

His father would want to know how he got out of the flat, and he'd have to reveal his secret passage. The door would be nailed up and he would be unable to get to his animals. They'd die.

The cub had relaxed against him, glad of company. It was lonely without its mother and its litter mates, and it was cold. It was warm inside Daniel's jersey and the offering of food had reassured the tiny animal.

If only it would lie quiet.

Daniel wriggled himself around so that he could see out of the entrance. He jumped as a small creature ran across the ground in front of him. Maybe a shrew or a mouse. He hoped it wasn't a rat, but he didn't think it was big enough. He saw a small body and a swift movement and then it was gone.

Were the men going to stay there for the rest of the night?

He relaxed as they moved, and then one of them turned and saw the tunnel entrance.

"That was where Mark Colley lost his Jack Russell last year," he said.

"Looks dangerous. Could lose other dogs down there." The second man bent down and stared inside. Daniel pressed his face into the ground. His hands were hidden. He hoped that he merged with the dark. He held his breath, and tried desperately to telepath the cub.

"Don't move. Don't whimper. Don't breathe."

"Black as a coal mine. Might be a good idea to block it. There are those cut logs on the other side of the ride."

Daniel lay still, horrified. They were going to seal him up. He ought to cry out. He couldn't. His voice wouldn't work. Maybe he could move the logs when the men had gone. He watched as the entrance grew smaller and smaller and finally there was nothing but the stifling dark that enclosed him with its choking smell.

Chapter Nine

The darkness was absolute. Daniel prayed that his torch would light, and that he had not broken the bulb when he dropped to the ground. The dim light revealed a small cavern, the entrance black, not even a gleam from outside. He pushed against the logs, but the men had fixed them firmly and pushed upright stakes into the ground to hold them in place.

The crack at the back of the cave was narrow, not big enough for more than his arm. He examined it carefully. The cub was asleep, tucked safely inside his jersey. It was earth, not rock. He had his penknife with him, a small enough thing, but sharp. He used it carefully, prising out earth, enlarging the hole.

He seemed to have been there for hours, but the luminous face of his watch told him it was only half-past three. He had to get out. He had to get back. He had committed every crime he could. He was out alone at night. He had the foxcub that should have died. Nobody knew where he was going, or what he had planned.

Would police dogs scent him through the logs?

The torch was fading fast. He had forgotten to buy a new battery. The little pile of earth was about the size of a molehill. At this rate he'd be here for the rest of his life, and die of starvation, so it wouldn't be a very long one.

The thought of starvation reminded him that he was hungry. He had half a chocolate bar in his pocket. He switched off the torch and sat and ate it. He was sleepy, but he must not go to sleep, whatever happened. The warm cub stirred inside his jersey. He had to get out. If they found him with the cub it would be taken away from him and killed.

There was time to think. Too much time. He had always been impatient with his father, with his mother, with Jake. Take care. Mind where you go. There's always danger. He had never thought that danger could touch him. Awful things only happened to other people.

Quite suddenly, he saw life from his parents' viewpoint. They weren't preventing him from enjoying himself. They were trying to keep him safe. Not because they despised him, but because they cared about him.

His father's warnings weren't nagging. They were based on experience and common sense. He wanted to run home to hug his parents, to tell them he was sorry he had been so stubborn. That he now understood their caution.

Maybe it was too late. He might never be free again. He might die here underground and maybe no one would ever know what had happened to him. It was all his own fault.

Please God, he said to the darkness. Let me get free. I won't be so stupid, ever again. Please help me. Please.

It was no use lying there, making no effort of his own. His grandfather's words came back to him. God helps those who help themselves. There would be no sword from heaven cleaving through the darkness, causing a landslip that freed him. It was up to him.

The tunnel narrowed towards the back of the cave itself. It had been possible to reach in with his arm. It was not possible to crawl through as he was far too big. Daniel had to come out at the quarry end as the tunnel entrance was now blocked.

No one had needed to dig all the way, as the terrier had been in the passage and not in the cave. The opening in front of him was impossible to crawl through. It was no more than a crack, big enough for the vixen, but not big enough for him. Suddenly desperate, he hit the wall, just beyond the crack. To his amazement, it crumbled under his fist.

He began to dig with both hands, working feverishly. The earth fell away, and his torch, shining on bare ground, revealed feathers and picked bones. He was inside the lair, and beyond him the entrance showed lighter, a faint lifting of the darkness. Wind brushed his face and teased his hair. The vixen had used the back of a large cave, big enough for a crouched man. She had laired in part of the tunnel. There were fallen wooden props which must have once have shored the roof, though it was a long time since men had quarried here.

Maybe the men who dug the terrier out had shored the roof as they went in.

He was through, and crawling to the ledge. He was standing, breathing the clean night air, listening to sounds which had been distant and muted and were suddenly clear. Far away a car changed gear and grumbled up a hill. A plane shot across the sky, its navigation lights bright.

His bitten hand throbbed. It would be hard to clean, as the wound was full of earth. He hoped it wouldn't infect. He might get anthrax. That was one of Anna's fears.

The ground was slippery from the rain. The

earth above the shelf was loose, but there was a bush within reach. If he pulled himself up by that . . . if it stayed firmly in the ground . . . he could . . . maybe . . . reach the top.

It was crazy. He ought to wait for light, and hope they would come to look for him. But why would anyone come here? He crouched, unable to move, fear of falling dominating every other feeling. Far below him were the deep waters of the old quarry, which never gave up its dead.

He longed for home, for his bed. It would be a long time before he went adventuring again at night. Jake was right, it was stupid. Daniel pretended that Jake didn't really know anything, but Jake knew he saw vans and cars in the woods.

Dig his toes into the soft ground and hang on tight to the bush. Daniel held his breath. Was it firm in the ground? Would it take his weight?

It did not budge, but he had not realised it was thorny. He bound his handkerchief around his hand, and tried again. Painfully, he pulled himself up until he was standing with his feet in the bush, the thorns pricking his legs through his jeans.

Another few feet to the top of the quarry. The vegetation here was dense, and he used the thick grassy stems to anchor his feet. Once he slipped, and lay flat, clinging to the ground. If only Jake would come by, offer him a strong hand and pull him clear.

He found a firm foothold on rock and levered himself up again. Inch by slow inch, the top coming nearer. One slip and he would face eternity. If he moved sideways there was a small tree at the top. Was that safely rooted? He didn't know, but he had little choice. He edged along the slope, and grasped the thin trunk.

Almost 5 a.m. He lay on the ground for a moment and then rolled fast, well away from the edge of the quarry. A bird cried over his head, startling him.

The approaching rustle and thump startled him. He could hear the pad pad pad of feet. There was nowhere to hide. He dared not stand and run. He lay quite still. Perhaps he wouldn't be seen.

The big badger passed him, pausing to sniff the air. Daniel lifted his head. The cub whimpered and the animal paused, staring, as if trying to identify the sound. Daniel stood up, and the badger moved swiftly across the ground, vanishing some yards further on.

Curious, Daniel walked over to investigate. The earth was newly dug, the soil fresh, and there were pawmarks. Cubs here too. He wondered if

Jake knew of the sett and hoped the badger baiters did not.

There was a hint of light in the sky. He had to hurry. There would be no time for sleep now. He was due up at six to feed the pups and he had less than an hour to settle the cub. He wondered if it were weaned. If not, he'd need a bottle. And milk. They had powdered puppy milk, but could he get at it without his parents knowing?

There was no spare cage for the cub.

Problems overwhelmed him.

He crouched down, and lifted the tiny creature. It had become used to him, and this time did not protest. Daniel's hands stroked the soft fur very gently. It looked at him with wise eyes from a small face topped with pointed ears. He could feel the beat of the tiny heart under his hands.

It lay still, trustingly. It felt thin, and he hoped that it was strong. It had to survive. And then what? Time enough to think of that later. Anna always planned everything, hoping to overcome obstacles that often never appeared. Daniel hoped for the best and somehow muddled through. As he had tonight.

Though even now he felt sick as he thought of the men sealing the tunnel, and his struggle to free himself. Forget it. He had work to do.

He slipped into the undergrowth beside the fountain and down into the tunnel. It was quicker than walking through the woods and climbing into the ballroom. The house was so immense.

By the time he reached the priesthole it was light enough for him to see without the now useless torch. He would have to creep along the tunnel, using his hands to guide him. He dared not go into the flat by the yard. All the dogs would bark, especially if they smelled the cub.

The bitch lifted her head. She was hungry and Daniel meant food. She accepted the bowl and began to eat eagerly. He sat, watching her. He had left the cage door open as she could not escape from the priesthole.

The cub had smelled milk. It was squealing. Daniel took it out from under his jersey and held it, as it tried to wriggle free. What on earth would it feed on?

The bitch, hearing the agitated cries, came to Daniel and nosed the cub. Daniel watched her anxiously. Suppose she killed it? It lifted its own nose towards her face, greeting her as it greeted its mother. She took it in her mouth, and tucked it against her, allowing it to suck.

Was the problem really solved? Daniel

watched her lick the youngster. She went back to her pups and lay down, and the cub followed, tucking himself in among them, accepting them as he had accepted his own brothers and sisters. One of them nosed him, and he licked its ear.

Daniel yawned, a face-splitting gape that almost hurt. He closed the outer door of the priesthole. He felt along the wall for the cherub's head that released the inner door and then he was through, the faint light of his torch showing the steps down.

He was almost at the bottom of the flight when the torch battery died.

The darkness stifled him. He was aware of the reek of the bats, and of their movements as they flew back to roost for the day. Wings brushed his hair. There was a constant squeaking, a sound which neither of his parents could hear.

Were there rats in the tunnels?

Daniel counted the steps. It was worse than being blind, he thought. Or was it like sudden blindness, no time to get used to the lack of landmarks? If he took the wrong opening he would land in the cellar under the kitchen, and his father might be up and hear him. He could not walk quietly in the dark. He bumped into things he had forgotten existed. An empty wine vat, its contents drunk long ago. A can that he had left down there, and forgotten to remove. He kicked it and it rolled, clanging as it struck a stone coping.

Sounds from outside were trapped here and echoed eerily. The dogs began to bark. The milkman bringing the day's supplies. How on earth was Daniel going to stay awake all day? Luckily there was no school for another week.

He stumbled against the first step of the flight that led to his own sanctuary. Ten steps, and then feel for the switch. The door opened, revealing his own room, the dawn light faint outside the window.

He was safe.

He touched the swan's head and the gap in the wall closed. He had examined it time and again, and it was impossible even to see the faintest line that revealed the door's existence. The markings in the panelling hid it completely.

He needed a shower. Would his parents hear the water running? He had to clean the bite and dress it. He stripped off his muddy clothes, wondering where to put them. The bathroom was beside his own room. His parents' door was some distance away. He could hear his father snoring.

Another half hour before the alarm went.

The warm water was bliss. He turned the

switch to cold, to wake himself up and gasped as the icy needles hit his body. A quick towelling, clean clothes and he was ready for the day.

He went into the kitchen and boiled the kettle, making himself a mug of strong black coffee.

He added sugar, and raided the fridge for a pasty. If he began to fry bacon his parents would wake up.

His mother, appearing in her dressing gown, stared at him.

"Are you all right?"

"Why wouldn't I be? The dogs woke me when the milkman came and I thought I'd better not go back to sleep again." He yawned, uncontrollably. "It would be nice to sleep till ten!"

"Not something anyone can do in our job." Jennie Murray poured hot water on to instant coffee, stirred the cup and sat down.

"Your father was out almost all night. There were poachers in the Owl Wood. And the RSPB man, who is guarding a nest with peregrine eggs in it." She smiled, her expression rueful. "I think your father would pay men to steal those eggs. The birds take his chicks."

She looked sharply at Daniel.

"What have you done to your hand?"

" I got bitten."

"By one of our dogs? What were you doing?"

"No, Mum. Not one of ours. There was a bitch running wild at the edge of the field. I think someone had dumped her. I tried to catch her, but she bit me, and disappeared."

It was a safe enough story, and was partly true.

His father came into the kitchen, wearing boots and trousers, but no shirt.

"So you're up, are you? I need a day's work out of you, my lad, and no sloping off at all. Do you hear me?"

Daniel did hear him with considerable dismay, as the bitch needed food and water, and the priesthole would need cleaning. And when would he find the time?

"I don't know why I was blessed with a useless son who never pulls his weight around here. You know as well as I do how much there is to do. I thought you and Anna would be back yesterday – but no. Off you go without any thought for the fact that your mother and I have to work every hour God made, and a few He didn't."

He glared at his son and walked out, slamming the door behind him.

Daniel sat staring at it. He could never please his father. It wasn't worth even trying. He would run off and live in the priesthole and Anna could bring him food, and his parents would never see him again.

He would be a hermit in the woods, living with the animals.

He had forgotten every fond thought he had had for his parents while he was trapped.

He hated his father.

Chapter Ten

Daniel stared unhappily at the two poached eggs his mother had put in front of him.

"Jake's back," she said. "Your father met him this morning. He took his mother to stay with her sister."

That meant that at least he need not worry about feeding the ducks.

Life was becoming more and more complicated. His father was never at his best after a night spent watching for poachers. He was sure that Sly had been out with his sons. Sly Cooper didn't see why anyone should own birds that flew free. Ken Murray had found cigarette stubs just beyond the pheasant coops. He was tired and short-tempered, and Daniel would have to take care not to upset him further.

Daniel was worried. In a few days they would be back at school, and the problem of feeding the bitch and her pups and the cub would become even greater. He might have to share the secret of the inner priesthole with Anna.

He would have to take Jake into his confidence.

He finished his breakfast hastily, gulping the last mouthfuls. He was very worried. He began to see his father's viewpoint. The bitch and her pups were a major responsibility. He could never leave her without food, and as the pups grew they would need more food, and a handful or so from his father's stock would not be nearly enough. Daniel began to think very hard.

Responsibility. That was what his father's job was about. Responsibility for working well and breeding good gundogs; his reputation depended on that. If he won at the gundog trials, then the pups fetched better prices, as their parents were obviously so good. Daniel had never thought about that before, either. His father had to please the old Lord and he was a very hard taskmaster.

Responsibility for rearing the old Lord's pheasants, for keeping them safe from their many enemies. Responsibility for arranging and managing the shoots.

The old Lord was very angry if anything went wrong, and if it did, his father would lose his job. Then how would they survive?

Suddenly, Daniel had responsibility. If he didn't feed their own puppies, his father or mother would. But no one but he knew about the foxcub, not even Anna. Nor did she know how to open the inner priesthole. Even though she watched, she didn't know just what it was he did to make the hidden catch work.

They would soon need dogfood in quantity. He hadn't nearly enough money saved to buy that, though he knew Jake would buy it for him. But he didn't want to ask Jake to spend his own money when it was Anna and he who were responsible.

Responsible. It was a frightening word, and he had never before realised exactly what it meant.

He had intended to slip down the tunnel before his father started the kennel work. A normal day began at 6.30 a.m. after a cup of tea. Breakfast was at eight, a heavy meal for a man who had already done several hours' work.

There was no chance of leaving now. No opportunity to ring Anna.

Unexpectedly, his mother provided a solution. She followed him as he walked into the yard. His father had already fed the dogs and the pups and was pushing a barrow containing two sacks of dogfood towards the feed store. Daniel looked at them, wishing they were his.

"Daniel chased off a stray bitch yesterday,"

she said. "She was wandering round the place. She bit him. I'm taking him to the surgery for an injection and to get the bite dressed. Can't do with an infected hand."

The wound was throbbing. Did foxes carry tetanus, or some awful disease that might make him really ill? It was only a baby, after all, but the bite was deep. Lucky it was his left hand.

Ken Murray looked at his son's injury.

"Be as quick as you can." His voice was grudging. Then his attention sharpened.

"Was she near my rearing pens?"

"Just beyond them. I did chase her right away," Daniel said. "She won't come back, I'm sure. She was too frightened. I yelled at her and threw stones."

It wasn't true, but he would have done if the need arose. He was at least certain she wouldn't be around outside. She was safely hidden and there was no way out.

"Good. So you do have some sense in you. Be as quick as you can. There's plenty to do around here and I need help. I've asked the old Lord for an under-keeper, but he says there isn't the money."

Money. Everyone seemed to need more than they had, Daniel thought. The small animals he and Anna had hidden in the ruins of the old house had never needed much in the way of food. But now there were growing mouths as well as an adult and very hungry bitch who needed extra to make her milk.

"I'm going to the supermarket afterwards," his mother said. He had not been listening to his parents' conversation. His own worry was flaring into panic and he wished his hand would stop hurting.

"I'll drop Daniel as near to home as I can, but he'll have to walk part of the way." His mother was walking away as she spoke, anxious to start her day.

She turned to Daniel.

"I had to make an appointment. We have to be there for twelve," she said. "Make sure you're washed and ready."

If only he could persuade her to drop him at the gates to the long drive he would be close to the fountain and could slip into the tunnel, up to the back of the priesthole and feed the bitch. There was enough for her morning meal and the pups and the cub did not need solid food yet. He guessed they were all about the same age, just over four weeks old. They'd need weaning soon.

If only they all kept quiet. But he knew they wouldn't. Little animals made a great deal of noise. At least the priesthole was soundproof but they couldn't stay there for ever.

He was not at all sure that Pete Cooper, the third of Sly's sons, who was in his form at school, did not know of the ballroom and its hidden animals. Sly had six sons and four daughters, and not one of them was pleasant. They all hated Daniel because his father worked for the old Lord. A gamekeeper and a magistrate. They were sworn enemies.

Daniel had no love for Pete. If Pete heard any of the animals he might well slip inside and harm them. He killed for the fun of it. Daniel had found a dead bullfinch two days before, and known it had been shot by either Pete or one of his brothers.

Pete, who was big for his age, and nastier than any boy Daniel knew, tormented any creature that he caught. That included other children at times, and once had included Anna. Daniel and two of his friends had lain in wait for Pete on his way home from school. Anna, hidden, had pelted him with conker cases, while the others held him still. That, Daniel hoped, had taught him a lesson. He had not bullied any of the four of them again.

There was enough food in the lunch box, which he had left just inside the tunnel, beyond the door, so that the bitch couldn't reach it. Modern dried foods made his illicit feeding much easier, as nothing went off.

He didn't want her bloated by eating too much in one meal.

He had better concentrate on his kennel work, or his father would be angry with him again. He could use his hand, although it hurt to do so.

His father's spaniel pups were seven weeks old and due to be sold, except for a handsome red and white dog with a merry nature that his father was keeping. They raced across the kennel as he brought in the food, crying noisily. The biggest, that Daniel had secretly named Mischief, intrigued by the bandage on his hand, leaped at it, trying to grab it.

A small Labrador bitch sat in the next kennel, watching them. She had come in for training the day before, and was to stay some months. She stared unhappily at the pups, missing her home and her owner and everything that was familiar. Daniel knew that within the week she would settle in as if she belonged, but just now she was lonely and in need of comfort.

"You can walk that one before you go," his father said, seeing Daniel bend and stroke the bitch's head. "She's had no training of any kind. Don't let her pull on the lead."

It was very soon plain that the little bitch knew nothing about leads either. She sat, terrified, as Daniel tried to coax her to walk. Gently, he persuaded her that life would be much easier if she did come with him, instead of behaving as if she had taken root.

"That's good, boy," his father said unexpectedly. "We'll make a dog handler out of you yet."

She walked a few paces, and then sat again.

"How do people do it?" his father asked of no one in particular. "Leave her till we have more time. She's nearly a year old and obviously never been on a lead at all. Never mind training her for gun work; she isn't trained to behave herself in any way."

Ken liked bold dogs, and had little use for those that were uneasy or nervous. Daniel made a sudden vow to himself that he would do the early training of this bitch. He knew how to make an animal trust him. His father knew how to make an animal obey him, and that did not always lead to a happy relationship.

"She's timid," Daniel said. "So I don't suppose she'll riot when she sees game."

"Don't you believe it."

One of the pheasants in the nearby pen suddenly honked. The gonglike note clamoured and then echoed, and Snipe barked. The cock flew from the ground to the tree branch that was put for them to roost, his brilliant fathers gleaming.

The little bitch was up at once, her face eager. His father was right. She was ready to chase if only she had not been enclosed in a kennel. She nosed the wire as one of the rabbits bounded into the sunshine, followed by a second, chasing him. They played tag for a few moments, and then vanished into the undergrowth.

"Lessons in the pen for you, my lady," Ken Murray said. "You can give some of them, Daniel. Time you took on some responsibility. No room for passengers in the big wide world. If you do well, we might get more dogs in to train."

Daniel looked up at his father, hardly able to believe what he heard.

Maybe if he trained the bitch, his father would let him have some of the money that was paid for teaching her. Sixty pounds a week for three months sounded like a fortune. Even twenty pounds a week would give him over two hundred pounds and he could buy a lot of dogfood with that. He'd open a savings account.

That would solve that problem without an argument. If he could gain her confidence and help her face the alarming world of humans, then his father could finish her training without upsetting her and cowing her. Usually Ken turned down the nervous dogs, but money had been tight in recent months. The old Lord did not always pay his father's wages on time. His mother was talking of keeping hens and selling the eggs, and of digging out the old pond for geese that could be sold at Christmas time. There were already six turkeys in a pen at the other side of the old house, and she was planning on buying in more.

She made and sold jam and marmalade and chutney and pickles. Her pies sold in The Feathers at lunch time and she could never produce enough.

"Did you hear what I said?" Ken Murray asked his son. "For heaven's sake stop daydreaming."

Daniel rallied his thoughts.

"I'd like my own dog," he said. "But not to train for the gun. We could do displays with them for charity.

"You and who else?"

"Anna and me. We've talked about it a lot. Her dad has promised her one of the next litter of collie pups. She's going to learn to train him for sheep."

"Talk never got anyone any place," Ken Murray said. "What you need, my son, is a sense of responsibility. I haven't seen much sign of that yet. Leave it to me or your mother. Time you grew up."

Daniel felt his face flush. It wasn't fair. Then, quite suddenly, he realised it was fair. He did forget to feed the pups. He did forget he was supposed to clean the kennels. He did argue over little things, feeling other boys had all the time in the world for their own affairs while he was supposed to work in much of his spare time.

"I'll try harder, I promise," he said, determined to work so well that his father would be impressed by his efforts that morning.

Ken Murray looked at him, one eyebrow raised, as if saying, I'll believe that when I see it. He whistled to his Labrador, and the dog bounded up to him and sat, tail wagging, eager to be doing.

"He's due for some water retrieves. Practise his swimming," Ken said. "Trials in a few weeks' time, so the rest of the kennel work is up to you. Do as much as you can this morning and finish it off as soon as you get back from the doctor."

Three hours later, his arm sore from an injection and his hand stitched and the bite neatly covered with a small plaster, Daniel ran through the woods, and dived into the bushes at the edge of the fountain. Too late, he remembered that his torch battery was dead.

He should have bought one on the way home.

He turned back along the ride that led to the house. The path was familiar, so well trodden that it looked like an animal trail. The children used it regularly.

It was a gloomy day, the sky overcast, threatening rain later. The woods on such days were haunted places, where the wind rustled and whined, and jays screamed. A robin, perched on a bush, flaunted its red breast and chittered a warning as Daniel passed him. Somewhere near there would be a nest, with gaping mouths and hungry babies.

There was a rustle in the bushes. A pheasant hen stared at him. Beyond her he caught the movement of the downy black-striped chicks. Then she was gone, and the babies froze against the ground. No matter how hard he looked, there was no trace of them yet he knew they were all about him, crouching terrified, seeing him as an invading giant, threatening them.

He had to hurry, or his father would complain – or worse, stop his pocket money which he needed badly. He paused, and listened. There were footsteps behind him. Somebody coming along the path. There were never strangers in the woods during the day. He didn't want to be seen. Someone might wonder what he was doing here, might investigate the ruined house, curious.

He stepped behind a tree, and held his breath. "Anna!"

He was irritated. He didn't want her here, didn't want to share the cub, didn't want her to know. If any of the adults learned there was a foxcub being fed and housed, he would be removed at once.

"I didn't expect you."

"Your mother rang my mother and said that you had to help your father all day. I thought maybe you wouldn't have time to feed Sukie."

"That's a daft name."

"She's got to be called something. It's as good as any other name. What have you done to your hand?"

Daniel decided he would have to take Anna into his confidence. Between them they might manage the feeding. He was already late this morning, due to his father's need for help. He was beginning to realise that it might be imposs-ible to feed the bitch twice daily on his own, and clean out the room where she and the pups were kept. Even with the two of them, it was going to be difficult.

"I got bitten. It was my own fault. I thought you had to help at home," he said.

"Mum sent me with eggs for old Mrs Carter. She's sprained her ankle and can't walk far. Mum thinks I'm with her, as she's lonely, but her sister's come to stay for a few days. I'm not expected back for an hour or more. What did you do to Sukie to make her bite?"

"It wasn't Sukie. I went out last night, and found one of the cubs still alive. He bit me."

"You are nuts!" Anna said, exasperated. "Where is he now?"

"Sukie thinks he's another puppy. He took to her as if she were his own mother."

Anna stared at him, speechless for once.

"I need a new torch battery," Daniel said, as they walked together along the path. He glanced at his watch. "I don't have much time. I haven't had time to feed her yet. We can't cope without light."

Anna lookd at him thoughtfully.

"Then let's take the short cut. It'll save nearly half a mile. We've only been told to avoid it at night."

The little wicket gate was padlocked, but was

easy to climb. And then they were in a hidden path, forcing their way through dense undergrowth. Clouds had drifted apart and the sun shone fitfully, dappling the ground. Then the way darkened as clouds hunted across the sky.

The old cottage had been little more than a ruin ever since the children could remember. Its stone walls towered into the sky, the chimney breast higher than the rest of the place. The roof had gone long ago. Empty windows were overgrown with ivy. There was a stout new wooden building at one end. The ruin blocked their route, which lay through its centre, and beyond it, through tangled gardens and then through the field that had not been touched by man since before the children were born.

The villagers said it was haunted, and Daniel always avoided that path when he was alone. Even with Anna, he was nervous.

Once onions grew there, Anna's great-grandfather said. Such onions as you never saw today with giant bulbs and a taste that defied description. Nothing like this supermarket pap that had no taste and no smell and might as well be made of plastic.

A shadow fled across the ground. Daniel shivered and looked up and saw the peregrine that nested here. Nobody ever came, except for

Anna and himself, and their visits were rare. Suppose that ghosts walked by day? It was impossible to run fast through the overhanging branches that brushed against his face.

Beyond the old passage was a pile of tumbled stones that they had to climb to reach the hidden garden. There was clematis here, and overgrown rose bushes. Once it had been tended and loved, but was now like so much else today that no one cared about any more.

"Come on," Anna said, her voice impatient. "We can go round the edge of the onion field."

There were no onions now. Only long grass and sorrel growing high and ragged robin in the hedges that had shot into the sky. The last occupant of the cottage had been famous for her jam and chutney making and her pickled onions were always sold in the local pub. Everyone referred to her as the Onions Lady and in the end everyone spoke of the cottage as the Onions. Maybe his mother one day would be remembered as the Pie or the Pickle Lady.

"My dad says the old Lord needs money," Anna said. "He's going to sell up. Your father may lose his job."

Daniel stared at her. She had turned to speak to him, ignoring the branch that she had just moved aside. It whipped back, stinging his face.

She walked on, unaware that her words had ruined the day.

Chapter Eleven

The sudden stinging hail reflected Daniel's mood. The children put their heads down and ran. The ground was slippery and it was raining so hard that they were soaked through in moments.

Daniel's thoughts raced. If his father lost his job, they'd lose their home. He'd lose a whole way of life. He couldn't imagine what other work his father could do.

The ballroom offered shelter. The sky was dark and the woods were dark. They climbed over the sill, brushing aside wet ivy.

The cages were empty now. Maybe one of those would do for the cub when he grew bigger. He couldn't stay for ever in the priesthole, nor could the bitch.

The cages were stacked against one of the remaining walls, where the children and Jake had rigged a shelter for them. Anna and Daniel stared in disbelief.

The six cages had been chopped up with an axe. The smashed remnants lay on the floor.

"Pete Cooper," Anna said. "I've seen him snooping round here a number of times."

"Why didn't you tell me? He might have harmed the animals if they'd been in the cages. I wouldn't have left any here if I'd known."

"There aren't any here now," Anna said.

"There could have been."

"And hippopotamuses could lay eggs." Anna was feeling as irritable as Daniel, who had been very poor company for the last twenty minutes.

Daniel grinned at her, suddenly amused in spite of his miserable thoughts.

Anna picked up a section of wood covered in mesh.

"There isn't a chance of repairing any of these. Wood and mesh cost money. And Jake might not make us any more."

"Jake'll be as mad as we are. Maybe he could have a word with Pete."

"Maybe your father could offer to shoot him," Anna said. "Nothing ever makes that creep behave. And I think it was Sly that shot your dad."

"Sly mostly uses traps and catapults. Guns make too much noise. It's the city gangs that come with guns. Thugs who don't care."

"Like the men who arrange dogfights and cockfights. Paul Smith at the boarding kennels said they had a dog there his dad reckoned had been used for fighting. So did the police when they saw it."

Daniel contemplated a world where people abused animals just for fun. He loathed bull-fighting, and the Spanish donkey festival when the poor beast was tormented. Humans weren't human. They were no better now than they were when old ladies had sat and knitted by the guillotine while heads rolled.

He pressed the cherub's head, and the priest-hole opened.

The bitch looked up at them. She was a pretty animal, her fur smooth and soft, her face and body brown and white, with a black patch over one eye which gave her a piratical air.

She had begun to accept Daniel, as he brought food, but she was not sure about Anna, whom she had only seen once when she was very frightened. She growled, deep in her throat.

Daniel went to the lunch box and opened it. He put the food into the borrowed bowl. The bitch watched him, forgetting Anna. She came out of her bed and walked towards the bowl. She began to eat greedily.

Anna stared at the puppies. The foxcub had disentangled himself from the litter and was stumbling towards them.

"I can see why you took him. He's wonderful."

The cub squeaked. One of the pups behind him answered, and he turned and made for the straw, cuddling down so that he blended amongst them, his small fox head hidden.

Anna squatted down to watch the little family. The bitch eyed her warily, but showed no other sign of worry. The pups and the cub huddled against her.

"We can't keep them in the dark for ever," Anna said, stroking the pups. They cuddled closer, wary of humans. The bitch thrust her way into the nest, and bared her teeth at them.

They began to feed, the little foxcub, slightly bigger than her own pups, pushing them out of the way, and fastening on to the teat with the most milk. For a few minutes there was no sound but a contented sucking. Daniel glanced at his watch. It was much later than he had realised.

"Dad'll skin me alive. Come on. I'll show you how to work the priesthole catch. I've enough food for two days here." He took a polythene bag out of his pocket and tipped the contents into the lunch box. "Will you do her tonight?"

"Sure."

"Can you bring food? Dad'll notice if we run

short too soon. He knows exactly how long each bag of dogfood lasts."

"Sure," Anna said again. "We'll have to earn some money. They'll soon be needing much more than that. I'd better see who wants babysitting."

She stood up and brushed straw off her jeans.

"I can probably slip away when you can't," she said.

The farm was so large that Anna could lose herself for hours at a time and no one ask where she had been. They assumed she was with the calves, or collecting eggs, or simply walking round making sure all gates were shut as there were footpaths through their land and holiday-makers and ramblers could be very careless.

Daniel watched Anna walk away before he slipped back into the priesthole and then into the tunnel. His thoughts raced, as he remembered that the estate might be for sale.

He thought all lords were rich but if Anna was right this one hadn't enough money to keep the place going. Perhaps they could turn it into a wildlife park with tigers and lions and bears.

Or restore the house and invite rich Americans for shooting holidays with his mother giving them medieval banquets.

He walked into the yard, where his father was

playing with the spaniel pups. They raced around him, and every few minutes he knelt down and called them. He was rewarded with a sprawl of pups hurtling towards him, climbing all over him, licking his face, while he praised them, and played with each in turn.

"Take over," he said to Daniel. "Took your time, didn't you?" He turned away and then turned back again. "Hand OK?"

"It's deep but not infected," Daniel said, grateful that his father had remembered to ask.

Ken Murray whistled to his two Labradors and leashed them when they came.

"Ten minutes with the pups. There have been summer visitors with loose dogs on the moor. If you take a dog out, leash it. We have to set an example and it's no use telling people off for rioting dogs when they see ours running loose. They don't have the control we do."

Playing with pups always put his father in a good mood.

"Anna says her dad says the Lord says . . ." he stopped, the sentence was getting out of control. "That the Lord might be going to sell up, as he hasn't enough money."

"So it's general talk, is it?"

"Is he? Where would we go?"

"He's thinking about it. Last year we hadn't

enough surplus game for any shoots at all. It was a very bad breeding year. Everything else seemed to multiply, except the birds. Foxes, stoats, weasels, crows. There's two peregrine families, and somewhere they say there's a kite, all feeding on our chicks."

"If you lose your job . . ."

"Put the pups away and let's have a coffee. It's maybe not all that bad. Anna won't know the half of it, nor does her dad." He unleashed the Labradors and whistled them to heel. They followed him and lay in the kitchen doorway.

The kitchen table was covered in a red and white checked cloth. The two covered plates contained scones and sausage rolls.

"I guess you're growing up," Ken Murray said. "It's so few years since you were a tiny boy, and before that a toddling baby. May seem a long time to you but to your mother and me it feels like yesterday and we forget you can understand now what goes on around you."

He spread butter from Anna's farm, lavishly, on two scones. Daniel preferred the sausage rolls.

"I know that we upset you by killing the foxes, but every year there are more of them. It's been a lot worse since hunting stopped."

He bit deep into his scone and chewed it.

132

"The countryside has to be managed. Mostly, it isn't. There aren't many landowners left with gamekeepers now. We knew about conservation long before anyone else. We help keep nature in balance. The people who make preservation orders on every animal simply don't understand that where man has destroyed natural enemies, he has to take over."

"It seems wrong to kill them," Daniel said.

"We don't; we cull them. Mostly we take the sick and the injured. Just occasionally, as last night, we have to take a few that are causing problems by wild killing. Blacktip has had more than eighty young birds in the past few weeks. Half of them he doesn't eat. He kills for the hell of it."

Daniel said nothing. He took another sausage roll.

"I have to make sure that each of my areas has just enough birds and nests in it. Too many and I get more of the predators coming in. If I keep it right, they don't bother us so much. But this year everything has overwhelmed me. I need another two men. Your mother does her best, but she has the house and shopping as well. Jake comes when he can but he has his own job."

Daniel looked out at the moors beyond the

edge of the wood. The trees ended just beyond their front door. He could see to the distant hedge that bordered Anna's farm fields, and then across to the rising hills that seemed to smoke in the distance. The two Labradors lay at the door, waiting for their master to change his mind again and take them out.

"The jobs are endless," Ken said.

Daniel suddenly realised that his father had never discussed work with him before because he hadn't bothered to listen.

"I get worried," Ken went on. "If this job goes I don't know how we'll manage. I'm not trained for anything else. With no other keeper to help me, I get overwhelmed. Kennel work and dog training; the endless inspection of the birds; the sick birds to nurse. In winter and spring there's the heather to burn off, so that we get fresh young plants and clean ground again. That's what keeps the varieties of plant that grow."

He paused and helped himself to another scone.

"If we didn't burn it there'd be nothing but bracken, overtaking everything else and killing all the other plants."

Daniel began to realise there was far more to his father's work than he had thought.

"The real trouble all the time is people," Ken said. "They trample everywhere and may disturb nesting birds. They pick wild flowers, and those become extinct. There's a patch of bee orchids on the sandy part of the moors. I've been guarding that very carefully."

The thought of a father who had no work to do worried Daniel immensely.

"Doesn't the old Lord care about the land?"

"He cares. But incomes go down and prices go up. He has my wages to pay; and everything I need to use costs far more than it did a few years ago. We lose birds and animals to poachers. City gangs. Not men like Sly. I can cope with him and his kind. They're stupid, maybe, a bit wily, but basically they just feel that anything on the land is for everyone, not just the owner of the land."

Daniel didn't want to interrupt his father. He so rarely talked about his work.

"The gangs are a new breed. Wild men who don't care about animals or people and will shoot just for the fun of it. No better than terrorists. Gamekeeper or policeman, they'll still shoot. They have no respect for the countryside, don't understand how it works, or that you don't shoot a deer before she gives birth; you don't shoot birds in the breeding season. I had hen pheasants killed last year and before I found the chicks they had been taken by the mink. And that's another thing."

Ken's voice rose angrily.

"The animal rights people letting loose creatures that don't belong in our country. The mink are breeding and killing off our native creatures. They'll make otters extinct. And they're dangerous. So are the coypu."

Jennie Murray's little runabout drew into the yard. She walked into the kitchen.

"I thought you were both working. And those scones and sausage rolls were for the W.I. Not for you."

Ken's face reflected his son's grin.

"Not now they aren't," he said. "I reckon they did us more good than the W.I. We work harder. Puppies, Daniel."

His wife looked at him and then at the empty plates, and laughed.

"Back to square one," she said. "And this time, hands off."

Daniel loved the puppy teaching. Spaniels had to range, keeping within calling distance of their owners, or they were out of hand and useless. Start with the pups, and they soon learned to come when called. They were never allowed to roam more than ten yards from

Daniel before he called them in. The small warm roly-poly bodies hurtled towards him each time he whistled, and he took them back to their kennel, feeling a tremendous sense of achievement.

Maybe he could think of a way the Lord could make money and not have to sell the place.

He glanced up.

The kite was overhead.

Even as he watched, it swooped on a shadow in the grass. Snipe was lying by Daniel's feet, watching her pups.

He pointed to the grass thirty feet away from him, where he knew a pheasant hid.

Snipe needed no further command. She was off, and the kite checked in its plunge and soared away towards the hazy hills. Daniel whistled the spaniel back. She came, her eyes alight with her success. The waving grass was still as the bird settled, safe.

Daniel returned to his work, his mind on the future. His conversation with his father had changed some of his ideas, and he knew now why Jake was so angry with him when he realised Daniel had slipped into the woods at night.

If he met men with guns and they saw him . . .

He had seen them and never considered the

thought that he might be a target and not the hares and rabbits and pheasants.

He shuddered.

The world felt, suddenly, a far more dangerous place. He and his family were as much at risk from the poachers as the birds were from the foxes.

It was not a pleasant thought.

Chapter Twelve

Pete Cooper hated school. He hated work, and he did his best never to read a book or write, unless a teacher stood over him and forced him to do so. He was in the remedial class, and resented the fact, but did nothing to improve his position.

He hated the world into which he had been born; the tiny cottage that was so small that he and his two brothers slept in a shed at the bottom of the garden. With two other brothers and four sisters and a new baby almost every year his mother had little time for any of them.

When his father was not in jail they fed well. Pete learned to read the woodland trails, to set nets for hares and rabbits, to charm a pheasant out of a tree. He learned to move like a drifting shadow, unseen and unheard.

He was a thin boy with a gaunt face, and eyes that stared unblinkingly at anyone who spoke to him. It was difficult to know if he understood as he rarely answered. His fair hair was long and dirty, and washing was something he did about once a week.

He lay on the river bank, watching a fat trout sun itself against a stone. His hands slid into the water, slid along the sleek torpedo like body, slid into the gills. A flip and the fish was out on the bank. A sharp tap on the head, and it lay still. He tucked it under his too-small jacket. It would help with the supper. His father was back inside, caught red-handed taking the Lord's pheasants.

Pete wasn't sure whom he hated most: the Lord or Ken Murray or Daniel. They were all rich, in Pete's eyes. Hunter's Keep fascinated him. He explored the old house when he should have been at school. He followed Anna, wanting to know what she did there and why she went so often.

He could never follow Daniel, who was like a ghost himself, materialising mysteriously from nowhere, and vanishing, knowing as well as Pete how to use shade and the trunks of trees, how to walk warily, never disturbing the twigs and bushes.

Both boys had seen the weasel dance his death dance, the fox and vixen courting, the magpies' rituals in the spring. Daniel watched for his own pleasure. Pete watched, ready to snatch food on the wing, or from the water.

Anna was unaware of the presence behind her, of the eyes that saw her go into the ballroom. Pete had chuckled when he found the cages. So they had animals here, did they. He smashed them, taking pleasure in destruction, and then wished he hadn't. If they kept rabbits, he could steal them and rabbit tasted good the way his mother cooked it. That was her only virtue. She knew how to turn the most unpromising of provisions into meals fit for a king.

They couldn't keep rabbits without cages.

Yet Anna still went to the ballroom, and climbed inside and vanished. Pete did not dare to follow her, and he could not see what she was doing.

There were boughs thrusting through the empty windows. Ivy grew thickly over the bare walls. Anna would never notice extra greenery.

Pete cut thick branches and stacked them in the corner, making a dense hiding place. He spent hours there, but Anna did not come. He made himself a hide above the farm and watched for her, stalking her as if he were a hunter and she a deer he intended to kill.

One evening he saw her leave the farm and turn into the woods. He was a shadow behind her, a rarely glimpsed movement, alarming a hunting weasel, but his quarry was unaware of his presence.

Anna moved without fear, in well-known territory, never scenting danger. Pete left her trail, knowing she was making for the Keep, and hid himself among the branches.

Anna was late and she was also tired. She was anxious to get home again before it was dark, as she had not brought a torch. She was not supposed to go through the woods at night, but the farm and the Keep were over a mile apart by road.

She pressed the cherub's head and the door of the priesthole opened. Pete stared, excited. A secret room. He heard the pups squealing. He saw the bitch come out and nose Anna's leg.

Puppies!

If he could find out how she had opened the door, he could take them, in a week or so, and sell them. He needed a sack. Maybe he could get twenty pounds each for them. How many were there? Six? Ten? He had known a bitch have eleven and even fifteen. Fifteen twenties: it was a sum he could not even reckon if he had paper and pencil but it was a lot of money.

Even five twenties was a lot of money.

Anna slipped inside the priesthole and shut the door. Daniel always kept a torch beside the food. She reached up to the shelf he had just fitted. It was more convenient than the shelf in the tunnel. Anna did not know about that. She had no idea there was another opening to the priesthole.

The bitch was hungry. She now accepted that humans meant food, and both Daniel and Anna were welcomed. The pups knew that and came for a cuddle. The foxcub was as friendly as his companions and climbed on to her knees as she knelt. His small body smelt musky, even now.

She would have to ring Daniel and tell him they needed more food. The pups were exhausting their mother. She ate greedily, always wanting more. Anna had brought her goat's milk and mixed it with some of the food into a mush to see if the pups would lap. The foxcub did. He was older by a few days, but the little animals did not seem to know what to do. Anna tried pushing the gruel into their mouths. They swallowed, but it was too slow a process.

Pete left his hide and went home.

Anna came out of the priesthole, closing the door carefully behind her. She went home, unaware that Pete had seen her, had seen the priesthole, and also the bitch and her little family. He had not seen the foxcub.

Over the next two days he made plans.

He chose a night with a ghost moon that hung like a Christmas token in an inky sky. Clouds hazed the dark, and all but a few of the stars were hidden.

Nobody would be about, he was sure. Even so, he moved with caution, not wanting to meet any of his father's cronies, who might be out after their own interests. The pheasants were everybody's game. It was a few weeks' short of the start of the shooting season.

He saw Ken Murray pass. Ken did not take the dogs out with him at night, though he was toying with the idea of asking the Lord to buy him a German Shepherd, a well-trained guard dog that would be of more use than his gundogs.

But with his job in jeopardy there was not much chance of that. The dog would be company. Ken hated the midnight woods since the time he had been shot. He listened for footsteps, and walked warily, but he did not see Pete.

Pete had brought the light they used for lamping, shining the torch to dazzle the rabbits and hares, who then stood still to be killed. He followed Ken, and watched him go into his flat, and heard the bolts drawn across the door. No one would be out till morning. He had all the time in the world.

He made his way cautiously back to the

ballroom and climbed inside. The torch lit up the carvings. Anna had stood there and must have pressed something. He tried to shift the wall, but it defied him.

An owl flew past hooting, and he jumped, and turned, and his elbow hit the cherub's head. His broad grin widened as the door slid open. The bitch came to greet him, and smelled danger. She raced at him, snarling, and he whipped round and into the priesthole.

The pups were stirring. He bent to pick them up. The bitch fastened her teeth in his hand and he swore at her, trying to shake her off. He moved away, and she let go, and ran a few feet from him, standing between him and her pups, determined to guard them with her life if necessary.

He picked up a branch and stripped it with the knife that was part of him, leaving a heavy cudgel. He hit out at her. She dodged, ran in and nipped his calf. He turned, tripped, and fell. She raced at him, and, as he tried to stand, to avoid her snapping teeth, his foot caught the lever that closed the door.

He was trapped.

Two pups had ventured out before the door closed and were outside, but the rest were in. Pete had no time for them now. He crouched against the wall, terrified, as the bitch flew at him again. His lack of movement puzzled her. She crouched, and stared at him, her eyes never leaving his face. She had sheepdog ancestry and this was a sheep she had to master, and teach it not to defy her. She had no intention of letting him go free. Every time he moved she snarled, and he thought she would pounce again.

As long as he didn't move she remained still. He put the torch on the ground, hoping it would last the night. He had no idea how to open the door from the inside and there was no clue to tell him that he needed to put his hand into a tiny, almost invisible, cavity and turn a small lever twice to the right.

There were four pups. Four twenties, if only the bitch would leave him alone, but she was fury on four legs and had no intention whatever of letting this stranger near her litter.

Pete had no watch, and no idea of the time. It was well after midnight, but there were long hours to dawn. Someone must come. The bitch was being fed. That was why Anna came here every day.

He saw the lunch box. Maybe it contained her food, but he dared not even try to reach it. He huddled against the wall, and presently he slept, with his enemy watching him intently, her low growls waking him when he moved a hand or foot, or his head.

She had bitten him badly on his arms and legs. He was aware of pain that grew worse as the night went on. He was cramped and miserable, and he was afraid.

The night seemed endless, but at last he was so exhausted that he slept.

He started awake when the back of the priesthole opened and Daniel stood there, shining his own torch. Pete's now shone so faintly that it gave very little light.

Daniel stared, shocked to find anyone inside the priesthole. Pete was so terrified that he offered no threat. Daniel shut the doorway behind him, putting his hand behind his back to operate the switch that closed. He had no intention of letting Pete see how the mechanism worked. The poacher's son could do little harm here, with the bitch ready to attack again. That she had already done so was apparent from the bloodstains on the other boy's clothing.

"How did you get here?" Daniel was almost speechless with shock. The priesthole was no longer safe. It was unlikely that Pete would keep his knowledge to himself, and if his father found the hiding place, he might find the tunnel behind, and then the way would be open to their flat.

"Anna let me in."

"I don't believe you. You followed her. Where is she? Have you hurt her? If you have, I'll set the dog on you."

Pete could not endure that thought.

"I didn't hurt her, honest. I followed her. I came in here after she went home. I wanted the pups to sell. I saw her open the door to this place. I tried all the carvings till I found the right knob. But I couldn't get out when I'd got in. I'm hungry and she's bitten me badly. It hurts."

"Good," said Daniel, without any sympathy whatever. Pete had all he deserved.

Daniel frowned.

"I'm calling the police."

He didn't want to. He wasn't sure that Pete had committed any more of a crime than he and Anna had. It would reveal the hiding place; it might reveal the secret tunnel; and it would also be impossible for his father not to know about the bitch and her pups and the foxcub. He glanced into the nest he had made for her. The straw was disturbed, and he could see only part of the litter. He walked over to investigate.

The foxcub was missing.

Chapter Thirteen

Daniel didn't know how to control his anger. All that effort wasted. One of the pups was also gone.

Did Pete know about the cub?

"Please don't call the police. I won't be back, I promise."

He cast a vicious glance at the bitch. Her eyes shone in the torchlight. "Not with that devil there."

"What have you done with the other pups?"

Daniel had to know if Pete has seen the cub.

"They ran past me. Two of them. They were outside when the door shut."

Pete was almost crying. He ached and the bites throbbed with pain and he was hungry and thirsty.

Daniel leaned against the wall, feeling behind him for the secret catch. He didn't want Pete to see it. If the other boy was afraid of being trapped again maybe the priesthole would be safe.

The door opened and Pete leaped up. The

bitch raced at him, but Daniel caught her as she ran to attack and held her.

"Get out. If you dare touch either of those pups I'll tell the police about tonight."

Outside, in the derelict ballroom, with the bitch held firm by Daniel's hands, Pete felt safe. He grinned.

"My word against yours."

"How will you explain those bites? You need to get a tetanus injection or you'll get lockjaw. Those are deep and will get infected."

"What's lockjaw?"

Daniel had seen a horse die of lockjaw.

"You get stiff, and then you get sort of fits, and your jaws grin and won't shut. You can't eat and you get worse until you die. You'd better go to the doctor, fast."

"You're having me on."

"I'm not. My dad has injections every few years because he works with animals. So do farmers and people who work with horses. I have them, and Anna. We wouldn't dream of not having them up to date."

Pete stared at him, his eyes frightened.

"Are you going or do I set Sukie on you again?"

Pete went, followed by threatening growls as the bitch tried to reach him.

Daniel took her back into the priesthole and gave her her food. It was some time before she settled. She nosed the pups, as if she were counting heads, and then began to seek around the room, looking for the missing pair.

Daniel closed the door. He hoped she was safe enough for now. He went outside and whistled, hoping the cub and the pup would hear his voice and answer it. He would need to come back here with one of the dogs. Maybe they would find the little animals. Where in the world had they gone?

They were small enough to fall victim to stoat or weasel, to hunting hawk and diving kite. They had had no lessons from their mother to guard them from danger, and they were unprotected. He looked around the ballroom, and stared miserably at the acres of wilderness beyond. An oak tree dripped acorns every year, and later there would be sweet chestnuts that he and Anna took home to roast in the ashes of the fire.

He looked helplessly at the tangled brambles and thick coppice, at the smothering ivy and the impenetrable thickets.

He heard a small whimper from beyond the ballroom and ran.

He couldn't place the noise. It seemed to echo

from the broken walls. It died away and then started again, the sound of a pup in distress, calling to its mother.

It came from the fountain.

He raced towards it.

There was a pipe, long disused, blocked at one end, that once had brought water from the stream. Once it had sloped uphill, but it was now broken, and lay adrift, pointing downhill, ending in a smother of earth.

Daniel shone his torch into its mouth.

There, far below him, four eyes reflected the light. The cub and the pup, terrified by their adventure, had taken shelter, and were trapped. There was no way he could reach them on his own. If anyone could. He would have to find Jake.

Daniel's thoughts were bleak as he ran through the woods towards the sanctuary. He should not have slipped away as soon as breakfast was over, but he had not intended to be so long. He would be in trouble for not coming to help with the kennel work. but that was unimportant now. It was a good job it was Saturday.

He had to rescue the pups. He had to find another home for the bitch. He had no idea how he could do either.

Chapter Fourteen

Daniel needed help. He could not imagine his father having any sympathy at all. He needed Jake. There was no way he dared keep the secret now. Pete Cooper might be back. Hopefully he was scared enough to go to the hospital and get the bites treated. But if he reported a dangerous dog, then the bitch might have to be put to sleep. She had bitten him badly, but it had been Pete's fault. He had no right to enter the priesthole. He had no right to touch her. She was not his property, and he had intended to steal the puppies.

His thoughts whirled as he ran through the woods, not caring this time that he made a noise. It seemed to be twice the distance to the sanctuary. If only Jake was there. He might be anywhere. In the woods, looking for nests to mark on his map. Making a note of the badger setts and the fox earths. Down by the lake, with the ducks.

He might not be there at all. He had been able to return quickly as his aunt went to stay with his mother. They had not needed to feed the ducks for him again.

Daniel raced on. No use going to his father for help. Ken would be angry. He had little time for stray animals, and he certainly would not accept a cross-bred bitch into his ménage. Both the rescue kennels in the village were full. Anna's father only kept collies. There was no room in the boarding kennels. They were always full of boarders and their own dogs, and had to turn clients away.

Ken would be furious when he heard about the foxcub.

The cub and pup were both trapped. Would it be possible to move that pipe, and free them? He couldn't do it alone. He wasn't sure that it would be possible, even with Jake.

If only Pete hadn't interfered . . .

But he might as well wish there were never tides in the sea. The Coopers were as difficult and unpredictable as nature, his father often said, and Daniel now realised what he meant.

Also, he could not forget that his father's job was at risk. If the Lord did sell the estate the old manor might be knocked down to make way for modern houses, and he and his family would be homeless. He knew they could never afford to buy a house.

"Daniel, you look as if the end of the world is at hand. Life can't be that bad?"

He hadn't seen Jake, who was walking towards him cradling a tiny duckling in his hands.

"I've just rescued this little one. He managed to get trapped in the wire mesh."

Daniel didn't know where to begin his story. "Jake, can you help?"

"Probably, if you tell me what sort of help."

"We rescued a stray bitch. We hid her and her puppies and Pete Cooper followed Anna and found her and wants to steal the puppies, only she bit him."

"Hold on, I'm getting out of breath," Jake said.

"I need a new home for the bitch. So that Pete doesn't find her. And two of the pups escaped. Well, one of them isn't a pup. It's a foxcub. And they're stuck in a pipe in the fountain. I can't reach them and they can't get out. Pete frightened them and they ran off and hid."

"Right," Jake said. "Let's find some tools. Spade, for one thing. And a saw."

Daniel nodded, almost dancing with impatience. Suppose Pete came back while he was away? And suppose he poured something down the pipe? He would hear the trapped babies squealing.

He raced ahead, feeling rather like one of his father's dogs, always impatient to be off, but constantly checking that the human it was with was still following.

There was no one by the fountain. Daniel wanted to go down the tunnel and check the priesthole, but the cub and pup might die if he wasted time. He shone his torch into the pipe and saw the two pairs of eyes reflect the light.

Jake looked down, and then sat on his haunches, considering the pipe and the mound of earth in which the end appeared to be buried. He began to dig, shovelling great spadefuls, throwing the earth on a heap.

"With luck, the pup and the cub are at the broken end of the pipe and if we clear away the earth, we can get them out easily," Jake said. "Otherwise I'll have to saw the pipe so that I can reach in, and that will terrify them even more."

Daniel was digging the earth with his hands, willing Jake to hurry.

Metal suddenly clanged on metal.

"There's something here. It isn't the pipe."

He put down the spade and loosed the soil carefully with his hands. Daniel began to help him, feeling metal against their skin.

A head appeared, and Jake brushed it clean with his handkerchief. A wise bronze head, with curling hair, with long slanting eyes, and lips that were pursed around a pipe. Jake brushed it clean with his handkerchief.

He stared at it in disbelief.

"It's the Mendoza Pan," he said. "Dear heaven! I can't believe it. There must have been a landslip and it was buried in the fall."

"What's so wonderful about it?" Daniel asked. Jake was staring at it as if he had found the crown jewels.

"Mendoza made a number of garden statues for the aristocracy in the seventeenth century. There was once a whole set of them here. The old Lord told me about them. Just recently they have become valuable. One sold for nearly half a million pounds at Christie's last year. He thought that if only the statues had survived the war they'd have saved the estate."

He set it down on the ground, handling it as if it might break at any moment.

"This is treasure, Daniel. Hunter's Keep has kept many secrets in its time, but this is the best yet. I wish we knew where the others were. Perhaps they were sold."

"There's more of them in the Folly," Daniel

said. "Lots of them, buried under bramble and nettle and Mum's Russian vine. I thought they were old rubbish someone had thrown away."

Jake stared at him.

"We'll have to tell his Lordship. Daniel, do you realise that if what I think is true, the estate may not have to be sold? This could be our salvation."

Daniel hadn't realised that Jake, too, might be out of work if the old Lord did sell his property.

"That'll have to wait," Jake continued, but his voice was still excited. "First, let's see if we can free the cub and the pup. We'll clean Pan up later, and then go and find the rest of them. We'll have to take him with us; someone else may recognise him and guess his worth. The recent sale was in all the papers."

Daniel stared at the little statue. Two cloven hooves and goat legs. They needed to clean it, to free it from soil, but for a moment, looking at it, Daniel was touched with a feeling of magic. At any moment the Pan would dance away from them. He was life incarnate, so vital that he made the two of them seem almost ghostlike by comparison.

Jake worked on, and at last came to the hidden part of the pipe. He dug the soil away carefully, and Daniel discovered that the end was indeed broken off, and had been buried. It was blocked with soil.

Within a few minutes Jake was able to reach in and pull the little animals free. He took the pup and Daniel took the cub and tucked it inside his anorak. It snuggled up against him, delighted to be out of its prison.

Jake lifted the Pan figure.

"Show me where the Folly is."

None them had seen the old Lord come into the clearing. He had been watching them for some minutes, frowning, and now he came forward.

"What have you there?"

Daniel jumped and stared up into the red face with its bushy white eyebrows and yellowed moustache.

"We've found the Mendoza Pan, my Lord," Jake said. "We had to free two little animals that were trapped in the old fountain pipe. The statue was buried under a mound of earth."

"The Pan? The Mendoza Pan?" The Lord sounded as if he couldn't believe his ears. "Let me see."

Jake set the little figure down. The Lord looked at it.

"I remember him when the fountain played,

when I was a small boy. I thought he was magical then. He still is, even half covered in soil. Look at those eyes and mouth. At the delicacy of the pipe. It isn't even broken." He walked around it, his eyes shining with delight. "Just look at the little cloven hooves and the goat's hair on the legs. The carving's incredible; it's so real. He'll jump up and dance for us in a moment . . . look at him, poised to fly. There used to be so many of them . . ."

He ran his fingers over the discoloured bronze.

"The Four Seasons; and the Twelve Months of the Year. Then, when my grandfather died, they vanished."

Daniel cleared his throat.

"They're all stored in the Folly. At least, there are a lot of them there. Little figures like this, buried among the weeds. I thought they were just some old rubbish; garden statues nobody wanted."

"They'll have shifted them during the war. Metal was commandeered to be made into weapons. All the railings went. Though they weren't nearly so valuable then, my parents loved them and wouldn't have wanted them destroyed."

He sighed, and then turned to Jake.

"Carry him for me. He's too heavy for me. Man, do you realise what this could mean? If they are all there I don't need to sell the estate. I can spend money on the sanctuary; can get another keeper to help Murray . . ."

He looked at them and his craggy face was softened by a delighted smile.

"Lead me there, boy. What are we waiting for?"

He slashed with his stick at a dandelion head, sending the little seeds floating on the air.

"Are you sure they're still there? Not damaged? Not broken?"

"I haven't looked."

Daniel wanted to check on the bitch, but there was no time now. He dared not reveal her presence. He tucked the cub inside his jersey, hoping the little creature wouldn't make any sound. If it did maybe the old Lord would think it was just another puppy. Jake had slipped the pup into his pocket. Its small face looked out with interest at this new view of the world.

Daniel's uneasiness grew by the minute. He was afraid that while they were away Pete would return with his brothers and have another try at stealing the pups. Three of them might take a stick to the bitch and beat her off.

Jake was talking eagerly to the Lord, both of

them making plans. Suppose the old man realised that they were using the ballroom? He must know of the priesthole. Suppose he wanted to go and look and remember the days when the house had been whole and he had lived there as a boy?

Maybe he too had explored the hidden passages. The worry wouldn't go. The two men were eager to reach the Folly, which was on the other side of the house beyond his mother's garden. Daniel suddenly wondered how it must have felt to live in that house, with its enormous rooms, with twenty-two bedrooms, with a ballroom and a picture gallery, with a kitchen that must have entailed hours of walking just within its walls and a huge scullery, the servants' quarters and the cellars and attics.

One thing, the ruins were so extensive that they would lead the old man away from the danger point. The Folly was a long way from the fountain. Maybe the old Lord didn't know of the tunnel exit; in any case he wouldn't look for it now, with others watching him, though he might come back later.

It would be quicker to take the short cut through the onion field, past the old ruin. Jake had recently turned the end of it into a store room, a secure room without windows, with a raised floor and a stout door, where he intended to keep surplus feed away from the rats. It was still empty.

Daniel, anxious suddenly to see the statues and make sure they were unbroken, ran ahead. It was too good to be true. It was a miracle. Yet all these old houses had treasures and the garden statues in the stately homes had been made by men whose names were now almost as revered as those of Michelangelo and Leonardo da Vinci.

He ran through the archway of the old garden that surrounded the ruined cottage. His mind was busy with plans. He almost choked as a hand went round his neck, and a knee was pushed hard into the small of his back. As the hand released his throat he yelled as loudly as he could.

He was staring into the eyes of Ben Cooper, Pete's elder brother, who was three times as mean and nearly twice as heavy as Pete. He twisted and saw that another brother, Deke, held him.

"We want that bitch," Deke said, his voice rough. He twisted Daniel's arm as he spoke. "She needs shooting. Setting her on poor Pete!"

"I didn't set her on. She was only defending her pups."

"Don't give us that." Ben had a knife in his hand and was holding it close to Daniel's face. Deke had gripped him by the throat again. Ben didn't see the old Lord creeping up behind him. He yelled as the stick came down on his right arm, and the knife dropped to the ground.

Daniel suddenly realised that the old man was not as old as he had thought. He was also very strong.

Jake held Deke, securing both hands behind his back.

"So," the old man said, stooping to pick up the weapon. "Threatening with a knife. Assault. Lucky not to have grievous bodily harm added to the charge."

He glanced around him and the two youths stared at him. The Lord was a magistrate and every villain in his area was afraid of him as he thought the punishment should fit the crime.

The old man looked around him.

"We can put them in your new store room. Take a tank to break out of that," he said. They were at the edge of the onion field, in the garden of the derelict cottage. Jake's store room was at the edge of it, only a few yards beyond the arch.

"Not there! It's haunted," Deke said.

"Good. I hope the ghost terrifies you," said the old Lord, thrusting his captive towards the ruin. Jake opened the door and the two were bundled inside.

"Don't try hammering, or you'll bring the old stones down. Been like that since the thirteenth century and they aren't cemented; just balanced. Not very well."

The door slammed shut.

"All right, boy?" asked the old man, looking at the marks on Daniel's throat. He rubbed them. They hurt. Deke had not been gentle.

Daniel nodded. He led the way more slowly, afraid that at any moment figures would explode from the bushes, as Pete had so many brothers, and a father as well.

The Folly was a tangle of vine, not yet in flower.

"The old Folly. I'd forgotten it," the Lord said. He tore away some of the clinging stems, and ducked inside. A moment later he exclaimed as Daniel's torch shone on the piled-up bronze figures.

Together, he and Jake began to untangle them from the brambles and weeds, and bring them out into the sunshine.

"Summer, Winter, Autumn, Spring," the Lord said reverently as the four saw the sunlight for the first time for many years. "Mendoza made them in the early seventeenth century.

They were commissioned by the family. I suppose that must have been my great-great-great-grandfather. Even in those days they cost a fortune. Nobody ever dreamed, when my parents were alive, they would become treasures almost beyond price."

He caressed Spring's bronze shoulders.

"Fifty years they've been here. The last place I would have thought of looking. I'd forgotten its existence. The vine hides it almost completely."

"I found the door by accident when one of the dogs started foraging in here," Daniel said. "My mother said the vine had been planted long before we came. That was just before I was born. Nearly thirteen years ago."

The old Lord was unable to believe his eyes, and touched the figures over and over again as if afraid they would evaporate.

"They probably stored them here in 1939, in the hope that they'd be safe. Just as well, as they'd have been damaged when the house was hit. Blast does strange things. We all thought they'd been lost in the bombing."

He stared at the statues.

"That war had a lot to answer for. Far more civilians died than soldiers and it was safer where I was at the front than in Britain with the

Germans trying to destroy morale by bombing any target they could. No one worried much about hitting only military targets and the bombing was never accurate."

"No satellites then to spy out the factories that made munitions," Jake said. "My grandfather told me it was all very hit and miss. You could go to bed at night in a shelter and go out in the morning and see your neighbours' house split in two, and people you spoke to yesterday were dead."

"I remember coming home on leave and seeing shops with no windows in them and notices saying 'Business as Usual'." The old Lord was still caressing the statues. "Food was short then too. We fed well in the army but when we were home on leave we had to eat like the rest of the country."

He sighed, remembering days so long ago that Daniel found it difficult to believe the old Lord had been alive then.

"It was a very nasty war, and went on for six long years." Unexpectedly, he laughed.

"Such silly things one remembers. We had no eggs – only dried eggs, which were quite unspeakable. They weren't bad in cakes, but tasted awful scrambled or in omelettes – like eating yellow leather. My mother made something called Polperro Pasty, which was a pie made with tinned pilchards. It was disgusting. That was on my last leave before the house was bombed. No servants by then, as they'd all been called up to the forces or the factories."

He stroked the Pan lovingly.

"My mother loved this little one." He sighed again. "It's so long since she died. The war changed all our lives; it changed the world for ever."

"My grandfather was in Coventry," Jake said. "They almost flattened that. No one who was born after the war will ever understand what those six years were like, he says. I find it hard to imagine. No lights at night in the streets, every house blacked out, so that not a glimmer shone through the curtains. Planes fighting overhead at night, and people as likely to be hit by bits of falling plane as by bombs or by shrapnel from the anti-aircraft guns that were everywhere."

Daniel looked at the statues, not wanting to think of war. It was unimaginable.

"I knew they were here," he said. "But I didn't know they had any value."

"How would you, boy? They've not been seen for fifty years. Neither you nor your parents were born when they were hidden. I was away from home, fighting in the desert. I was taken prisoner. When I came home I discovered both my parents had died the night the house was hit. I had no home. There was no one to tell me that the statues had been hidden. I thought they'd probably been blown to smithereens by the bombs. Two fell on the house. They probably thought so big a building must be important, and maybe house troops. There were evacuees. They died too."

Daniel looked at the figures. They were unimaginably old. The Four Seasons were as delicately made as the little Pan. Spring with her hands full of flowers; Summer garlanded; Autumn holding a horn of plenty, full of ripe fruit; and Winter stark in a cloak, as if sheltering from the snow.

The old Lord took his handkerchief and dipped it in a puddle and wiped Spring's face, revealing gentle features and laughing eyes. She was dancing, as light and dainty as the little Pan, but far more human.

It took another hour to unearth all four. They stood in line, the little Pan leading them. They needed cleaning; they needed to be restored to their former beauty, but even with some earth still clinging to them and the green discoloration of centuries, Daniel could see that these were special.

"I could sing, I could dance!" the Lord said and turned as Daniel's father came into the clearing, two Labradors at heel.

"Your son has found the secret of Hunter's Keep." The Lord sounded like a different person, his voice full of excitement. "I don't suppose you've even heard of the Mendoza statues. They've been missing since the war. One like them sold recently for half a million pounds. I've been dreaming of finding them. We've unearthed five already and I believe another dozen are still under all this greenery."

Ken Murray stared at the little figures. It was hard to believe that they could be so valuable.

He swallowed. He was unable to think of anything to fit the occasion. His mind was whirling, unable to realise that his job was now secure.

"They'll need storing safely," he said at last. "If anyone gets wind of them . . . Though they have been safe enough here all these years. No one knew anything about them. I've never seen them before."

"They'll fetch a fortune." The Lord still couldn't believe it. "No need to sell the estate. I can get a man to help you, Murray. If they make enough, I'll get two. Restore the place to some of its old glory."

"How did you find them? What were you doing?" Ken Murray asked his son.

"We found the Pan first. We had to dig out the fountain. Jake guessed what it was and I told him about these. Anna and I found them ages ago when we were exploring. We just thought they were old things that nobody wanted and had put there as there was nowhere else to store them and they weren't worth selling. Like the old stone statues all over the place."

"Why were you digging in the old fountain?" Ken Murray asked.

Daniel hesitated but knew he'd have to confess.

"Anna and I had a bitch and her pups hidden in the old ballroom, and Pete found them and one pup got out, and so did this." He removed the foxcub out from under his anorak. His father stared at it as Jake took it. "I found him after you killed the foxes. He escaped. That's when we found the Pan."

"It's bound for my sanctuary, and then on to Gloucestershire where there's a man who has a reserve for foxes," Jake said. "Daniel was looking after it for me, and also looking after the bitch we found. It's a long story, but the cub was running from Pete Cooper and got trapped in the old fountain. When we dug to free him, we found the Pan buried under a mound of earth."

Daniel cast a grateful look at Jake.

"And then I remembered finding the other figures when I was exploring the Folly," he said.

"I think we should celebrate," said a voice from the edge of the clearing. Daniel's mother stood there, a tray of glasses in her hands, with orange juice for Daniel and home-made wine for everyone else. "I've been eavesdropping."

She laughed.

Later that day Daniel showed the Lord and his father the tunnel system and the priesthole.

"I didn't know it was still in working order," the old man said. "I used to hide down here when I was a boy."

Jake had taken the bitch and her pups and the foxcub back to his home. Anna had homes for the pups and Jake intended to keep their mother.

"Pete Cooper knows about the priesthole; he could find the tunnel," Daniel said.

"We'll seal it up," the Lord said. "I wouldn't like to think of people being able to get into your home that way."

He walked away, suddenly looking taller, his head held high, as if a load of worries had slipped from his back.

Daniel looked at his father.

"Would you like to come down the passage before it's sealed up?" he asked, hesitating, afraid his father might say no.

Ken Murray smiled at his son.

"Let's go," he said. "I imagine it's pretty spooky down there all alone. I'm not sure I'd have been happy exploring it by myself. I hope you're going to stay in at nights now unless you're with me or Jake. There's danger out there."

Daniel knew that now. He felt as if he had learned a great deal in the past few weeks. His father's big torch lit up the passages, taking away all the fear.

"For all that," his father said, as they neared the end of the passage, "if it hadn't been for you, I'd have lost my job. His Lordship would have lost the estate and we would never have found the Mendoza statues." He sighed. "It's just as well I didn't know what you were doing. I'd have been worried sick."

They climbed out into the moonlight, Daniel feeling a suden rush of affection for his father. They stood side by side, listening to the soft owl calls.

"Next time you feel a yearning to go exploring by night, come with me," his father said. "I'll be glad of company. I like the dark, too. There's so much wildlife to see. I don't only want to shoot it, you know. I love learning about the creatures that live amongst us."

It was a new thought for Daniel.

They climbed out of the fountain and sat on its rim, looking up at the moon. A fragile new moon, with a star in its arms. Daniel did not need to wish. His wishes had come true.

No need to leave Hunter's Keep, which he suddenly and passionately felt to be his home. He was part of the place, and he was needed, as his mother said, to help keep the show on the road.

He looked up as a shadow fell across them.

"Jake!"

"I thought I'd find you here. The last time. That particular secret will be lost for ever. Hunter's Keep certainly hid more than we thought, didn't it?"

Daniel nodded.

"The old Lord asked me to give you this. She's out of the best stock in the country and you can found your own line with her."

He saw his father's sudden grin, and knew that this was no surprise to him.

The tiny pup fitted trustingly into his cupped hands. He looked down at her, at her bright eyes and her spaniel ears. She licked his chin and wriggled companionably until she was comfortable, tucked against him as the foxcub had tucked against him. He couldn't believe it. He'd wake up and find he was dreaming.

A springer spaniel of his own; a pup to train, maybe to compete with in the gundog trials.

"What are you going to call her?" asked Ken Murray, holding out a finger to the tiny animal, who licked it happily, enjoying the attention these people were giving her.

"There's only one name she can have," Daniel answered. He held her close against him and she licked his hand.

"I'm going to call her Secret."